CLAIMED BY THE SAILOR

FIONA DAVENPORT

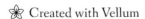

CLAIMED BY THE SAILOR

Silas Atwood met Phoebe Baker while she was in the middle of family drama, but that didn't stop him from recognizing they were meant to be together. The Navy SEAL planned to seek her out the next day, but a mission made that impossible.

When the hot sailor who helped her brother showed up on her doorstep a month later, Phoebe wasn't sure what to think. His timing turned out to be impeccable because she found herself in trouble again. And this time, Silas wasn't going to let anything or anyone stop him from claiming Phoebe.

PROLOGUE

SILAS

I spotted Command Master Chief Arrow Hamlin, one of my commanding officers, as I turned into a lot in front of a small apartment building. He stood by his big black SUV with a petite blonde looking up at him as though he'd hung the moon. Not that his sappy expression was any less pathetic. Okay, that might have been an exaggeration, but damn, the guys I worked with were dropping like flies. Although, if I was being honest, I couldn't blame them. They'd fallen for some awesome women, and part of me was a little jealous.

Pulling into the spot closest to Arrow and his woman, I parked and climbed out of the little car. It had broken down recently, which was how Arrow met Sage—because he pulled over to help her. The tires had been balder than Mr. Clean, so he asked me to replace them and return the car to Sage's apartment.

Once I was on my feet, I tossed the keys to Arrow. "Replaced all four tires, sir."

"Thanks, Silas." He pulled his wallet out of his back pocket and tugged some bills out to hand them over to me. "Let me know if this doesn't cover it."

Sage reached for the zipper on her purse. "I should be the one to pay."

Arrow's fingers wrapped around her wrist, stopping her as he muttered, "Didn't I prove to you last night that you're my woman?"

"You did," she admitted softly, looking down at the ground as her face bloomed with pink. I couldn't help snickering, which made her blush even more and earned me a dirty look from Arrow. I just grinned in return.

He turned back to Sage and continued, "Which means I get to take care of anything that has to do with your safety, including those damn tires that should've been replaced months ago."

"I wouldn't bother arguing with him, ma'am. He can be a stubborn motherfucker," I warned.

Before anything else was said, Sage's attention jumped to a small red car driving into the parking lot. A pretty redhead—who I assumed was Sage's roommate, Phoebe—pulled up to Arrow's SUV. The door opened, and a dirty, haggard-looking young man climbed out to wait for her.

Paul was Phoebe's brother. An addict who'd nearly gotten Sage killed by the dealer he owed ten grand. The guy had mistaken Sage for Phoebe and didn't give a shit when he realized she wasn't. Arrow had to put the motherfucker in the ground to get him to stay away from his woman.

Since Phoebe was her best friend, and Arrow would do anything to keep Sage happy, he was paying for Paul to go into rehab. A very specific rehab run by Jacob, a friend of Arrow's. It was incredibly strict, and Paul would have to work his ass off to get better, but if he did, he'd leave a changed man. After his little reunion with Phoebe, I was going to drive him up there myself and check him in.

Phoebe shut off her car, then jumped out of her vehicle and threw herself into her brother's arms. "Thank goodness you're okay. I was so worried about you."

Holy shit.

I was wrong. Phoebe wasn't pretty, she was fucking drop-dead gorgeous. She had stunning, clear blue eyes rimmed with dark lashes and plush lips painted red—conjuring up all manner of dirty thoughts. Even the smattering of freckles across her cheeks were cute.

She was perhaps six inches shorter than my six-foot frame, but she wasn't a tiny little thing like Sage. Phoebe was more of an average build, but she had curves that made my mouth water.

And that hair. Fuck. The copper locks were up in a messy bun on top of her head, but they were clearly thick and long. Her hair would be amazing when it fell all around her while she was naked, playing peekaboo with her big tits. I knew without a doubt that I would eventually know what those silky-looking locks felt like wrapped around my hand while I fucked her from behind.

I was drawn back to the present when Paul sobbed against Phoebe's shoulder. "I'm so damn sorry, sis. I never meant for you to be dragged into my mess. When I think about what could've happened to you..."

"I'm okay. They didn't get anywhere near me." She reassured him as she patted his back before stepping away. "Sage is the one you owe the apology to since she was here when they came looking for me."

Paul turned toward them, his gaze darting toward Arrow before he looked at Sage. "You will never know how much I regret that you got hurt because of the shit I pulled. I am so sorry, Sage."

Phoebe had been so focused on her brother that she hadn't noticed the small bandage and bruise on Sage's cheek until that moment, and she cried out, "You got hurt?"

"Only a little," Sage reassured her with a soft smile. "I'm fine now."

Phoebe's shoulders slumped. "I hate that you were hurt at all."

I glanced at my watch and calculated how long it would take to get to the rehab center before they closed. We needed to hit the road.

"Sorry to break this up." I jerked my chin toward the SUV. "But it's time for us to go."

"Where are you taking him?" Phoebe cried, clutching her brother's arm as he tried to climb into the passenger seat of the SUV.

"He's agreed to go back into rehab." Arrow explained how strict the place was and hope filled Phoebe's eyes.

She turned to me, her lashes fluttering, and ensnared me in her beautiful blue orbs for a second. "Thank you for helping my brother."

"My pleasure," I murmured, my voice thick with desire. There was also a promise in those two words.

A promise that she'd see me again, and then the pleasure would be all hers.

Phoebe's cheeks filled with a pink blush, letting me know she wasn't immune to the crackling electricity between us. I winked at her, and she ducked her head as her brother and I climbed into the SUV.

As we drove away, I glanced in the rearview mirror to see her still watching the vehicle. I knew I wanted her, but right then, I realized I'd bit the dust along with my teammates.

Phoebe was mine.

IT WAS WELL after dark when I returned home, and for the first time since I moved into my condo, I felt how empty it was with just me there. I'd only moved off base six months ago, but I was certainly glad I made the change since I intended to have Phoebe permanently moved in with me as quickly as possible.

I lay in bed for a long time, making plans for the next day. Grabbing Phoebe after work and kidnapping her didn't seem like the smartest idea...no matter how appealing it sounded.

Dinner was a safer bet. I'd take her out, and we

could get to know each other. I wouldn't push her, but I could still hope that we'd end up back at my place, burning up the sheets.

Eventually, I fell asleep, but my night was restless because I kept waking up hot and bothered by dreams about Phoebe.

The sun was barely cresting the horizon when I gave up and padded into my bathroom to take an arctic shower.

My cell was ringing when I stepped out, and I wrapped a towel around my waist before hurrying out to the bedroom.

When I saw who was calling, I sighed. A mission.

For the first time since becoming a SEAL, I found myself wishing I didn't have to go.

After receiving my orders, I called a friend who put me in touch with Jonah Carrington, who owned one of the best security companies in the world. He agreed to have eyes—female eyes—on my girl while I was gone. To protect her, of course. And to make sure no other males got anywhere near my Phoebe.

1

PHOEBE

Staring up at the brick building in front of me, I started to have second thoughts about coming here. It had been almost a full month since I'd last seen my brother, but I was still so angry with him over the trouble he had brought to my door because of his addiction. Paul had hurt me so many times before, but the pain had always been emotional—never physical. And none of my friends had suffered because of anything he'd done until his latest mess, getting in so deep with a drug dealer that he'd come looking for me and found Sage, my best friend, instead.

She had also been my roommate until she moved in with her new husband. As happy as I was for her, having her move out had sucked. I tried to look on the bright side, though. At least something good had come out of her being accosted by a drug dealer since she met Arrow when she fled our apartment.

Heaving a deep sigh, I grabbed my phone to call Sage. I had told her where I was going this morning, so I wasn't surprised when she picked up on the first ring. "How is Paul?"

"I haven't seen him yet. I'm still sitting in my car, wondering if I made the right decision coming here today." Pinching the bridge of my nose between my index finger and thumb, I heaved a deep sigh. "I'm not sure I'm ready to face him when I haven't forgiven him for what happened to you."

"Stop worrying about me and focus on what you need to do for yourself."

This wasn't the first time Sage had encouraged me to get over what had happened to her because of Paul's actions. She had somehow moved past everything when I hadn't been able to do the same. Probably because she had Arrow's support through it all while I only had my parents—whose loyalties were divided between my brother and me.

They'd already been up to visit him and had urged me to do the same. I knew they meant well, but I wished they could see my perspective a little more. "I'm not sure what I need, except for Paul to get his crap together so he isn't pulling our family apart anymore."

Sage's tone was gentle as she said, "Arrow checked in with his friend when we got back from our honeymoon to see how Paul is doing. From what he told me, it sounded as though he's making good progress."

"Yeah, when he called to ask me to come up, he sounded better than he has in a really long time." I let out another sigh. "But I've been here before, hoping for the best when he's in rehab and then being disappointed when his sobriety doesn't stick. I'm not sure I have it in me to do it all over again."

"You need to give yourself more credit, Phoebe," she chided. "You're a lot stronger than you realize."

Her encouragement was exactly what I needed to push through my fear. "You're right. I can do this."

"Of course, you can. Now quit stalling and get in there."

After we said our goodbyes, I tucked my phone into my purse and climbed out of my car. The next hour passed in a blur as Jacob, Arrow's friend who ran the rehab, walked me through the progress Paul had made so far and explained that he was going to stay for another thirty days.

"He really agreed to that?" I asked, stunned since

he'd always been ready to leave the minute his time was up whenever he'd gone to rehab before.

"He didn't just agree, it was his idea." Jacob reached over and squeezed my hand. "And I wouldn't be surprised if he chooses to extend his stay with us to ninety days."

My eyes widened and filled with tears. "Wow, you're a miracle worker."

He shook his head. "No matter how good our success rate is here, it's ultimately up to our patients to do the truly hard work. Which your brother has been doing."

"I am so relieved to hear that." I flashed him a watery smile. "Thanks for alleviating my concerns. I think I'm ready to see Paul now."

"Good." He patted my hand. "Although your brother was nervous about your visit, I know how much he's looking forward to seeing you and making amends."

Paul had reached this stage in recovery before, but his apologies were always vague and halfhearted in the past. I was happy to discover that was no longer true when I walked into a small conference room and he jumped up from his seat to rush toward me. "I am so, so sorry, Phoebe. I know I've said it to you many times before, but knowing that Sage got hurt because of me—that you could've been hurt or died—finally knocked some sense into me. I hate that it took me falling so low to see the harm my actions have caused, but I promise you nothing like this will ever happen again."

There was no missing the sincerity shining from his blue eyes, and I took note of how much better he looked. He'd put on some weight, his clothes were clean, and his skin had a healthy glow. "Do you mean you won't do drugs again?"

"I'm sorry, sis. I wish I could make that promise, but I will always be an addict, just one in recovery." Stepping away from me, he gestured toward one of the chairs, waiting for me to be seated before he dropped down next to me. "The struggle will be there for me each and every day for the rest of my life. Some days will be easier than others, but there might come a time when I fall. The only promise I can make to you is that I will do whatever it takes to stay clean. I'll go to meetings, call my sponsor, ask for help whenever I need it because I never want to let the people who love me down like this again."

"You really mean it," I whispered, sniffling at the overwhelming sense of relief that rushed through my body.

"I do," he confirmed with a nod, reaching out to

take my hand in his. "I know you've already given me more chances than I deserve, but I'm hoping you have it in you to forgive me one more time for all of the pain I've caused you. For lying and putting you in danger. For Sage getting hurt because of my actions. And for not being the big brother you deserve."

Only thirty minutes ago, I hadn't thought it was possible, but I found myself not hesitating to say, "I forgive you."

"Thank you." A lone tear rolled down his cheek, and I leaned over to give him a hug.

His arms wrapped around me tightly, and I gave him a moment to pull himself together before I let go. "Thanks for working the steps like you're supposed to. I'm proud of you, Paul."

"You–" He cleared his throat a couple of times. "You have no idea how much that means to me."

I appreciated that he wasn't trying to hide how my forgiveness impacted him. We chatted for a while before saying our goodbyes, and I felt so much better as we parted ways. It was hard to believe only a month had passed with how much he had changed. I felt on top of the world because I was filled with hope for my brother's future for the first time in years.

As I walked through the lobby, a woman who appeared to be about my age jumped up from a bench to the side of the front doors and stared at me as I approached. I flashed her an awkward smile and murmured, "Hello," intending to walk past, but she moved into my path.

"You're Paul's sister, right?"

I nodded. "Um, yes."

"I thought so." She grinned at me. "He mentioned in our group session that you were coming, and you look so much alike with your red hair and blue eyes."

"Yeah, it's pretty hard to miss that we're siblings."

"You're so lucky to have him for a brother." She looked behind me and let out a loud sigh. "I'm really going to miss seeing him every day."

"Oh, are you discharging soon?" I asked.

"Very soon." Her lips curved down in a pout. "Today, actually."

Knowing how difficult the transition to home could be from the other times Paul had rehabbed, I understood why she might be anxious about leaving. "From what I've heard, Jacob runs a tight ship around here. I'm sure you wouldn't be leaving if they didn't think you were ready."

"I know, but I was hoping Paul and I would be

discharged at the same time since we were admitted on the same day."

Her eyes gleamed as she said my brother's name again, and I realized she might have a crush on him. Feeling awkward, I mumbled, "Maybe it's for the best since neither of you is supposed to be in a relationship. The universe has a way of making sure things happen when they're supposed to, so perhaps you'll meet again in the future."

And for the first time in longer than I could remember, I was actually looking forward to finding out what the future held for Paul.

2

SILAS

"Damn, I'm exhausted," I grunted as I ambled out of the room where we'd been debriefed from our mission.

"Hooyah," my teammate, Kade, muttered in agreement.

The assignment had initially been a four-day op. Then shit went sideways, and it turned into four weeks. I desperately needed to sleep, but I needed to see Phoebe more.

When I hadn't been focused on my mission, she'd been on my mind constantly. I hated that I had no way to get in touch with her to let her know I was coming back for her or just to hear her sexy voice. When I could catch a little sleep, I'd dreamed of all the things I planned to do to her when I returned.

Before I could relax, I wanted to see her. Partly because I needed to know she was safe—despite the regular updates from Jonah. Although I got them in bursts because I couldn't check my email frequently. The other part of me wanted to make sure she was real and as beautiful as I remembered.

I figured I should call first, but I didn't have Phoebe's number. Luckily, Arrow and Sage had returned from their honeymoon while I was away. He'd been at the debrief, so I waited for him outside the entrance. The cool air felt amazing after the oppressive heat I'd endured for the past month.

When Arrow emerged, I pushed off the wall I'd been leaning against and walked toward him. "CMC," I called out.

He stopped and twisted around. "What can I do for you, Petty Officer?"

Arrow was one of my commanding officers, but he was also a friend. Off duty, we called each other by our first names—except when I called him "Sir" out of habit. However, it was funny that using his given name felt less natural than addressing him by rank.

"How was the honeymoon?"

He grinned and tucked his hands into the

pockets of his khaki pants. "Amazing. I love my job, but it was hard to come back after having my wife all to myself like that."

"I can imagine," I chuckled. Several weeks ago, that wouldn't have been true. But now, I only wanted Phoebe's undivided attention and a lot of uninterrupted time to explore her body. I clapped him on the shoulder and teased, "Knocked her up yet?"

Arrow's smile grew even wider, and I shook my head in disbelief. "I was joking, Sir. You seriously knocked up your wife on your honeymoon?"

"No. I took care of that before the wedding," he said smugly.

Laughter burst from my chest, and I had to bend over to catch my breath. When I stood back up, Arrow was still smiling like a loon with his chest puffed out so much I was waiting for him to pop a button.

I shook his hand and slapped him on the back again. "Congratulations, CMC."

"Thanks. Don't tell Sage, though. She wants to wait."

"No problem." I cocked my head to the side and studied him with a smirk. "How many other people have you told?"

Arrow looked away as he cleared his throat. "I'm guessing my honeymoon wasn't the real reason you wanted to talk?" he mumbled, avoiding the question.

"Good thing your friends all keep secrets for a living," I chuckled. "I was wondering if you'd been keeping tabs on Paul?"

Arrow nodded. "Sage was worried about his sister, so she talked Jacob into giving us regular updates on him for her to pass along to Phoebe."

"How's he doing?"

He shrugged. "As good as can be expected. Jacob said he's progressing and thinks Paul will turn things around. But it's a hard road."

"And his sister? Phoebe?" I tried to be nonchalant, but Arrow clearly picked up on something in my tone because he narrowed his eyes.

"Was this all your convoluted way of asking about Phoebe? My wife's best friend? Practically a sister?"

I was acting like I'd grown a vagina. But I was a fucking SEAL. We were straightforward and got shit done. So I stopped trying to be covert and laid it all out.

"There's something about her," I admitted. "I met her for all of ten minutes, and that was all it took to know she was mine."

Arrow rolled his eyes and rocked back on his heels. "Welcome to the club." Then he winced. "Damn, the timing of this mission really fucked with your relationship. It must have been hell being gone for so long without a way to stay connected to her."

"Merrick put me in touch with Jonah Carrington," I explained, knowing Arrow would understand my choice. Merrick Ashford had been a member of my SEAL team long before I came on the scene. Apparently, he'd taken the fall for a corrupt CO to save his teammates' asses. He'd become a hitman until he met his wife, Audrey. Now he did mostly security consulting, although he helped his friends out on occasion...when someone needed to disappear. We'd worked together a few times and become friends.

His wife was best friends with Jonah's daughter, so I'd taken advantage of the situation in order to keep me from losing my fucking mind while I was gone.

Arrow nodded. "Smart."

"Anyway, I figured I should call Phoebe before I just showed up at her house. Do you have her number? Or will you get it from Sage for me?"

"Sure." Arrow pulled his cell phone from his shirt pocket, then paused, his eyes shuttered as he studied me. His hesitation pricked my temper, but I didn't let it show.

"Before I do, I want to make something very clear. Phoebe and Sage are like sisters, which makes her family to me. I think you're serious about her, but if you break her heart, I'll kick your ass. Then I'll let Sage loose on you, and trust me, you should be terrified if that happens."

I was happy Phoebe had such good people in her corner who would protect her if I couldn't. But I was still irritated that he questioned my intentions, so I nodded sharply. "Understood, sir."

He fiddled with it for a moment, then mine vibrated. "I texted you her contact information but..."

I raised an eyebrow when he trailed off thoughtfully. "Sir?"

Arrow shook his head and a small smile curved his lips. "If I were you, I'd skip the heads-up and just show up at her door. Don't give her a chance to blow you off or turn you away."

I scratched my chin as I processed his suggestion. "Maybe you're right."

We said goodbye, and I headed home for a quick shower. Once I was clean, I threw on a pair of jeans

and a long-sleeve black Henley. After making my
way down to the building's garage, I got into my
SUV and headed to Phoebe's apartment.

On the way, I checked in with my parents,
brother, and sisters. I always sent them a text when I
left for an assignment, or they would freak out when
they couldn't get in touch with me. They were
always my first calls when I returned. Although from
now on, they would come after Phoebe.

It was early evening when I drove into the lot in
front of her apartment and parked in the spot next to
her car. I'd called the bodyguard assigned to her and
confirmed that Phoebe was home in case I had to
find her someplace else. Before hanging up, I
thanked her and asked her to send me a full report
once she got back to the office. I'd already told Jonah
I was back, so Phoebe's guard would head to a new
assignment the next day.

My anticipation to see her had been steadily
building, and it propelled my feet forward so I
quickly reached her apartment. I pounded on the
door, probably a little harder than necessary, but my
patience had run out.

"Okay, okay!" I heard an exasperated voice call
out. I grinned because even after only meeting her

once, I could picture her pretty face scrunched up in a cute little scowl. But as the lock disengaged, I wiped it from my face so she wouldn't think I was laughing at her and risk a bad second impression.

The door opened, and Phoebe filled the space. I was proven right—she had an adorable scowl on her face, and her hands were propped on her hips. "What the—Silas?"

She whispered my name before her jaw dropped in surprise. Then her cheeks turned pink when my mouth curved up into a grin.

"Hey there, beautiful. I'm happy to see that you remember me."

Her lips curled down, and she dropped her hands to her sides. "Well, I thought...it was stupid, but I was sure you would...but then you didn't...anyway."

I immediately picked up on what she was trying not to say, and I hurried to reassure her. "I intended to call you the day after we met, but I was called in for a mission in the middle of the night. I just got back this afternoon."

She sucked in a breath and double blinked before murmuring, "You were going to call?" Then she shook her head as if trying to clear it. "You just got back? And you're here?"

I laughed at her bewildered expression and placed my hand on her stomach before gently pushing her back into the apartment. "Can I come in?" I asked, despite the fact that I was already crossing the threshold. "I promise to explain everything."

3

PHOEBE

"Sure," I murmured even though he hadn't waited for permission to move past me.

It was so difficult for me to wrap my head around the fact that Silas was in my apartment. Although we'd met under awful circumstances, I'd thought there had been a spark between us. So much so that I had expected to hear from him at some point over the past month. Granted, I hadn't given him my number, but I was certain he could have gotten it from Arrow if he'd really wanted it. So when he never reached out, I assumed my feelings had been one-sided and tried to forget about him. Only that hadn't worked.

I hadn't been able to get Silas off my mind. The number of dreams I'd had about the dark-haired

SEAL was a little embarrassing, considering I usually woke up on the cusp of an orgasm. Remembering all the things I had fantasized about him doing to me with his tanned, muscular body made me blush.

His piercing green eyes scanned my face as he turned toward me, making my cheeks heat more. "I'm sorry I ghosted you for a month."

"I don't think it counts as ghosting when I didn't give you my phone number." I laughed softly, feeling so much better now that I knew he'd also felt the pull between us, and there was a reason I hadn't heard from him this past month. One I probably should have considered since I knew he was a SEAL. "Or when you were overseas on a mission and couldn't call me even if you had it."

"Yeah, well"—he scraped his palm against the dark scruff covering his cheek—"I still felt like shit not being able to explain why I disappeared after dropping your brother off at rehab. I meant what I said. I planned on reaching out the next day, but then we got called out on a mission and coming to you wasn't an option until now. That's why I came straight here after I left the base."

I didn't doubt that he truly meant that. He

looked as though he'd lost a little weight while he was gone, and his eyes had faint shadows under them. "You probably should've gone home to get some food and rest first. I could have waited another day."

"Maybe, but I didn't want to wait to see you. Not when you were on my mind the entire time I was gone." He stepped closer, and my breath caught in my throat. "The past month couldn't have been easy for you after everything that went down. How's your brother doing?"

My lips curved into a smile. "Better than I expected. I just visited him on Sunday, and he seems to be taking rehab more seriously than he ever has before. He decided to stay another thirty days, which is huge, considering he had always been ready to leave as soon as possible when he tried to get sober. I think what happened with Sage finally got through to him. He couldn't ignore the damage his addiction was doing to the people around him any longer."

"I'm glad to hear that, but I'm sorry you had to go through what you did for him to get serious about his sobriety."

I pressed my hand against my chest. "All I did was hide at my parents' house while Arrow took care of the problem. Sage was the one who went through the wringer because of Paul."

"Don't downplay what happened. You might not have been physically assaulted like Sage"—his fists clenched at his sides, as though just the thought of me being hurt made him furious—"but you weren't taking a vacation either. The situation was still difficult for you."

"It was." I reached out and squeezed his forearm. "Thanks again for taking Paul to the rehab center. I would've been a sobbing mess if I'd had to do it myself."

"You're welcome, baby. I just wish I'd been around to do more." He flashed me a sexy grin. "But at least I'm here now."

I glanced at the screen of my phone and cringed. "I am so sorry. As happy as I am to see you, I really have to get going. I have a networking event for work that starts in half an hour."

"Damn, my timing sucks again." His gaze dropped to take in the black jumper I was wearing, and his eyes filled with masculine appreciation. "Can I walk you down to your car?"

"That would be great," I quickly agreed, reluctant to part ways so soon. "I just need to slip on my shoes and grab my bag."

"Don't rush on my account. I'll take every minute with you that I can get."

Butterflies swirled in my belly as I darted into my bedroom to grab my black sling-back heels. After I put them on, I made sure my lipstick was in my purse and headed toward the front door where Silas was waiting for me. "Okay, I'm ready."

He placed his palm against my lower back as he led me out of the building, sending a shiver of awareness down my spine. "What kind of networking event are you going to tonight?"

"Nothing fancy. Just happy hour & hors d'oeuvres at a nearby hotel, mostly with event planners and people from the office. The goal is to schmooze them so they'll be more inclined to book events with us. I'm a marketing assistant for a local hospitality company that owns and operates a bunch of restaurants and hotels all over California."

Silas let out a low whistle of appreciation as he held the door and gestured with a sweep of his hand for me to go first. "Impressive."

"Thanks. It's my first real job since I only recently got my bachelor's," I explained, tucking a lock of my hair behind my ear.

"Beauty, kindness, and brains. You really are the whole package, Phoebe Baker."

Luckily, he knew which car was mine and was able to guide me directly toward it because my head was in the clouds over his compliment. It was also a good thing that he was much more observant than me since I would most likely have missed the piece of paper tucked under my wiper blade until after I pulled out of the parking lot.

"What's this?" he asked, his brows drawing together.

"Probably just a flyer for a local pizza place." I pulled the sheet off my windshield and turned it over, gasping when I saw how wrong I was.

Before I could fully absorb the threat that someone had left behind to warn me to keep my nose out of other people's business, Silas pulled the paper from my hand and growled, "What the fuck?"

"I...I...I don't understand," I cried, wrapping my arms around my middle and hugging myself tightly before Silas uttered another curse and pulled me against his chest. "Why would someone leave a note like that for me?"

"I don't know, but I'm sure as fuck gonna find out," he vowed, brushing a kiss against the top of my head.

I took the comfort he offered for about a minute before pulling away to stare up at him with pleading eyes. My hands were shaky as I gripped the front of his shirt and whispered, "This doesn't make any sense. I swear my life is normally drama free. In fact, I'm pretty boring compared to most people."

Gripping the corner of the note between his index finger and thumb, he shook his head. "Not sure you'll ever be able to convince me that you're boring, baby."

"That's only what you think because both times you've been around me, there's been major drama," I huffed as I tried to wrap my head around what was happening. "But my days are boring as heck. I haven't been at my job long enough to have moved past acquaintances to friends with any of my coworkers, and that's where I spend most of my time besides being at home or seeing my parents. Sage is the person I'm closest with, but it can't be about her because she's been on her honeymoon. And I don't see how Paul could be involved since he's been at rehab this whole time. The only visitors he had before I went to see him were my parents, and they'd never do something like this."

"I've seen more than my fair share of people doing fucked-up things for the strangest reasons. Don't try to second-guess everyone in your life, baby.

All it'll do is drive you up the wall. Besides, that's what you've got me for, to figure this shit out."

Silas had been wrong when he said that his timing sucked. It turned out that he was in exactly the right place at the right time to help me...again.

4

SILAS

My hand curled into a tight fist, wishing I could crush the note inside it. But that would further contaminate any evidence left behind.

"We need to bag this," I told Phoebe as I walked her back into the apartment. She grabbed a small plastic bag, and I carefully put the note inside and sealed it shut. Tomorrow, I would take it to a friend at a local lab and have it run for prints. Tonight, I would call Deacon and see if he could get his hands on the camera footage of the parking lot. Since his specialties were surreptitious entry and technical surveillance operations—and he was a wicked hacker —he was my best bet.

I turned to Phoebe, who still looked anxious, and tried to smooth out the scowl on my face so I wouldn't further upset her. "Don't worry, baby. I won't let anything happen to you," I murmured. "Why don't you relax while I make some calls—"

"I have to go to this work event," she sighed as she shook her head. "I'm still new, and if I don't show up, it could jeopardize my job."

I wanted to put my foot down and tell her she wasn't going anywhere, but this was literally only the second time we'd ever met or even spoken to each other. I didn't want to send her running before I had a chance to make her mine. If she knew just how deeply possessive I was of her already, she'd probably freak out and slam the door in my face. I didn't understand how my feelings had grown so out of control in such a short time, but there was no turning back now.

However, not being able to stop her from going didn't mean I had to let her go alone. "Fine," I agreed. "Only if I go with you."

Phoebe's eyes widened, and she shook her head again as she opened her mouth to say something, but I cut her off. "This is nonnegotiable, baby. Your safety comes first, and I'm not leaving your side until I know you're not in any danger."

My eyes swept over her from head to toe, once again admiring how fucking sexy she looked in her one-piece outfit that subtly showed off her delicious curves. *Focus, Atwood.* It wasn't super dressy, and her thick red curls were pulled up into a casual pony-tail, but I didn't think showing up with a scruffy guy in jeans would help her image.

Jerking my head toward her front door, I said, "We can stop by my place on the way. It will only take me a few minutes to change."

Phoebe's mouth opened and closed a few times as she processed what I said. I simply stared at her with an expression that made it clear I wasn't going to budge. I almost smiled in triumph when I saw a spark of excitement in her pretty eyes, and she nodded in acquiescence. Instead, my most charming smile spread slowly across my face, and I enjoyed the pretty shade of pink that bloomed on her cheeks.

"Get your cute ass moving, baby." I put my hand on the small of her back as we walked outside, then waited for her to lock up before guiding her to the passenger side of my SUV.

"I can drive," she protested. "I don't want you to have to bring me back—"

"Forget it, baby," I rumbled as I opened the door. "Remember what I said about not leaving your side?"

Phoebe swallowed hard and looked as though she might say something but lost her nerve because she pressed her lips together and allowed me to help her up into the seat without comment. I buckled her in before she had the chance and almost groaned when my arm brushed over a hard nipple poking through her clothing. I took a deep breath, but it didn't help since the air was filled with her mouthwatering scent. I quickly slammed the door shut and jogged to the driver's side. Once I buckled my seat belt, I started the ignition and backed out. As I pulled out onto the street, I reached across the console and laced my fingers with hers before setting our hands on my thigh. I asked her about her work and kept our conversation going as I drove so she wouldn't have time to dwell on what happened or overthink what was developing between us. It also didn't hurt that I wanted to know everything about her anyway.

When we arrived at my condo, I pulled into the garage and parked. "I'll be quick," I said before jumping out of the car and swiftly making my way to her door. I opened it and held out my hand.

"I can just wait here," Phoebe stated with an understanding smile.

I rolled my eyes and bent over to unbuckle her seat belt, steeling myself against the electricity that arced between us whenever we touched.

Taking her hand, I tugged her out of the vehicle and tucked her into my side with my arm around her shoulders. "How many times am I going to have to repeat myself?" I growled, letting the corners of my mouth turn up so she knew I was teasing. Mostly. "You're going to have to learn to do what you're told, baby." I paused, and my smile turned wicked. "I promise you'll like the rewards that come from being a good girl."

Phoebe's mouth formed a little O as she blinked up at me. While she didn't seem to fully understand what I was implying, I knew she had some idea because her clear blue eyes heated, darkening a shade.

We'd reached the elevator, so I swiped my card. When the door slid open, I ushered her inside. I was incredibly tempted to push her up against the wall and kiss her until she couldn't think about anything but me. My hands itched to feel her curves, and my lips tingled with the anticipation of feeling her mouth under mine.

However, I suspected that once I started, I wouldn't be able to stop. And I wanted Phoebe to know that everything about her was important to me, including her career. So it was best that I didn't get sidetracked by my hunger for her. It could wait. *I* could wait, I told myself—mostly believing it.

When the lift reached my floor, I kept her hand in mine as I walked off and down the hall to my door. Once I unlocked it, we entered, and I guided her over to the sofa. "Have a seat, baby. I'll only be a few minutes."

Her eyes bounced around the room with interest, and I chuckled. "Feel free to snoop. I have nothing to hide from you."

Phoebe's face registered surprise, but she also looked pleased. "I would never snoop," she insisted halfheartedly.

"I would," I admitted with a laugh. When she giggled, I couldn't resist bending over to place a swift kiss on her nose. That was all I allowed myself before straightening and hastily retreating to my bedroom.

After trading out my jeans for a pair of slacks and my Henley for a polo, I changed my shoes and headed back into the living room. When Phoebe's eyes landed on me, they darkened again, and a pretty blush stained her cheeks. "You clean up good, Silas," she teased.

I laughed and winked at her. "Ditto, baby. Although you would look sexy as fuck in a potato sack."

She giggled again and beamed at me. For a moment, I was lost in the beauty of her smile. Then I shook my head to clear away the fog, once again reminding myself that we would have plenty of time to indulge later. Forever, if I had my way.

"Let's get going, baby," I said as I extended my hand toward her. "Before I can't talk myself out of locking you up here until I know you're safe."

She allowed me to help her to her feet, and I kept us tethered by our entwined fingers. We headed out to my vehicle, and as we were driving out of the garage, Phoebe plugged the address for the hotel into my GPS. The destination was only ten minutes away, so we took the ride in comfortable silence.

As a SEAL, I'd been trained to handle situations that involved a lot of waiting, usually in complete silence, and often in less than desirable conditions. But I'd never been able to completely relax with anyone except my family. So I was astonished that being with Phoebe felt so easy.

The hotel was a flurry of activity when we arrived, which grated on my protective instincts. Then we walked into the ballroom, and my mouth curled down in a deep frown. The large space was opened on our end by several sets of double doors, and the wall opposite of us was made of floor-to-ceiling windows, broken up by three sets of doors—all of which were propped open to let in the night breeze—which provided access to the garden area. The exit situation annoyed me, but all the strangers mingling around the high-top tables set my teeth on edge.

I slipped my arm around Phoebe's waist and tucked her into my side. Several people called out hellos to her as we walked into the throng of guests. She tried to step away the first time, but I tightened my arm, making it clear she wasn't going anywhere without me. After that, she just waved and said hi in return.

Phoebe had explained that this was a networking event, so I knew I'd have to suck it up and share her attention while we were there. That didn't mean I had to be happy about the situation.

A buffet table of hors d'oeuvres sat in the middle of the room, and since she'd mentioned having missed dinner, I moved us in that direction. I was starving, but the protective instincts in me wouldn't let me take my focus off her safety.

When we reached the table, she handed me a plate but smiled gratefully and shook my head. She frowned and went to set both plates down, but I grabbed her wrist to stop her. "Eat something, baby," I insisted. "I know you're hungry."

"And you're not?" Phoebe remarked. "Didn't you say you came straight to see me?"

I nodded.

"I'm going to assume that means you didn't stop to eat."

"I'll grab something later. Go ahead," I urged, finally releasing her so I could nudge her along in line.

When she hesitated again, I took her plate and began to fill it until I'd piled it high with food.

Phoebe laughed. "I'll never be able to eat all that."

I shrugged and put my hand on her back again, steering us toward an empty high-top table. When we reached it, I drew her around to stand with our backs to the wall. That way, I had a view of the exits, the entire room, and everyone in it.

A few people Phoebe introduced to me as local vendors stopped by to chat about upcoming events. When they moved on to speak with someone else, my eyes narrowed on a preppy-looking guy who was probably a few years younger than me. He smiled warmly at my girl as he approached the table. His eyes practically devoured her, and I had to stamp down the warning growl threatening to rumble in my chest. I needed to wait to see if the little shit did something stupid. I wouldn't make a scene, but if he hit on my girl, he'd regret it.

"I'm glad to see you here, Phoebe," the kid said with a wide smile as he moved around the table and held out his hand. Before Phoebe could shake it, I grasped his palm, swallowing it up in my much bigger one.

His eyes widened as he glanced at my hand holding his in a firm grip. I was making a point, so I wasn't squeezing hard enough to cause pain...yet. "Hello," he greeted me, his voice pitched just a little higher than it had been when he'd first walked up. "I'm Blaine Asbury. My family owns the hotel," he added with the obnoxious arrogance of a spoiled, trust fund kid.

I nearly snorted at the name. It was pretentious and fit him perfectly.

"Silas," I muttered gruffly, tightening my fingers just a bit. Phoebe let out a little gasp, but I slipped my other arm around her waist and gave it a squeeze, letting her know I wanted her to keep quiet. When she didn't say anything, I gave her another squeeze to show her my appreciation.

"Oh, I didn't realize you were seeing anyone," he

said, his gaze bouncing between me and Phoebe. He was trying to extricate his hand from mine, but I was irritated that he was speaking directly to Phoebe, essentially trying to freeze me out of the conversation. It was so ludicrous, I almost laughed. Did he really think he had a shot with someone as incredible as my Phoebe?

"Well, now you know," I grunted.

"Is it serious?" he mumbled, his eyes darting in my direction for a split-second. This time I didn't suppress the growl.

"Of course it's fucking serious, Blaine," I snarled, putting an emphasis on his name with a disgusted tone. "Now run along and hit on someone else's girl-friend before I decide to kick your ass and save everyone the trouble." At this point, I put enough pressure on his hand to elicit a little girlie yelp from him. Then I finally released it, and without another word or glance at my girl, he scurried away with his tail between his legs.

"Oh my gosh," Phoebe groaned. I glanced down to see her face buried in her palms. Before I could say anything, she looked up at me, her pretty cheeks flushed with color, and snapped, "What was that?"

"A friendly warning," I muttered.

"Are you going to scare off everyone who comes

to talk to me? If so, it would have been better if I'd just stayed home."

I didn't feel bad for scaring away that little shit, but I would regret doing anything that would negatively impact her job.

"I'm sorry," I told her with genuine remorse. "I'll do better." I almost ended it there, but I figured she deserved total honesty. "But if I see another man undressing you with his eyes like that little shit, I can't promise I won't make it clear that if they don't keep their eyes to themselves, they'll likely be swollen shut tomorrow."

5

PHOEBE

I probably should have been appalled at what Silas just said, but I found myself impressed... and oddly turned on. Blaine Asbury was a colossal jerk, and I dreaded bumping into him, which happened often since the company I worked for managed several hotels owned by his family.

I always tried to avoid him when we were at the same events, but that wasn't easy when he seemed to seek me out each and every time. Not even having a big, intimidating Navy SEAL at my side had stopped him from coming over to flirt with me.

If I wasn't so proud of my job and didn't want to do anything to risk losing it, I would've let Silas's interaction with Blaine slide. And maybe even gave him a kiss for being so hot while he got growly over me. However, I needed to at least try to rein in Silas enough that we didn't get thrown out of the event. "First of all, Blaine can be creepy in his arrogant way, but I don't think he was undressing me with his eyes. And nobody else is going to, either."

"We're going to have to agree to disagree on that one, baby." Silas shook his head as he scanned the room before his perceptive gaze landed back on me. "I'm a guy too. I know what he was doing."

My eyes narrowed. "Because you spend a lot of time stripping women of their clothes in your head?"

"Only you, baby," he reassured me with a sexy smirk.

It was difficult not to lose my train of thought when his smile made me feel as though my panties were about to spontaneously combust, but I forced myself to stay on track. "Okay, then can you at least promise that you'll find a way to make your point without getting me into trouble with my boss?"

His grin widened as he nodded. "Challenge accepted. Hooyah."

"I'm going to take that as a yes." I shoved a phyllo cup with goat cheese and fig jam into my mouth and chewed while I considered how to word the last part. Deciding the best way was to just be direct, I asked, "Girlfriend?"

"Guys like that don't understand innuendo. If there's even an ounce of wiggle room, they assume there's still an in for them." We barely knew each other and this wasn't even our first date—even if it felt like one—but that didn't stop my shoulders from slumping at his explanation. Noticing my reaction, Silas added, "But I didn't throw that particular word out there randomly."

Tilting my head to the side, I asked, "You didn't?"

"Nope." He reached across the table and laced his fingers through mine. "I figured it's going to be true some day in the hopefully near future."

"I...I...I—" I stuttered, sounding the same as I had when I found the threatening note on my car, except this time I was stunned for a fantastic reason instead of an awful one.

He gave my hand a reassuring squeeze. "Relax, baby. I'm not going to pressure you into anything. We have time for you to settle into the idea of being in a relationship with me."

"Well, okay then," I mumbled, appreciating how he laid his intentions out there when most guys prefer to keep a girl guessing. "Let's hope we survive tonight with my job intact so we have the chance for me to do that while I'm still gainfully employed."

"You don't have anything to worry about, Phoebe. I won't let anything happen to you or your job tonight."

Silas kept his promise and even ended up helping me connect with several event planners—a couple of whom only came over to try to chat him up. I'd enjoyed being able to call myself his girlfriend both times since turnabout was fair play.

"That was fun," I murmured as he led me out to where he'd parked his SUV.

He chuckled and shook his head. "I'm glad I could provide some entertainment."

"Hey, you can't really blame me for warning off those women when you're the one who started it," I teased.

"Don't take me wrong, I'm not complaining," he reassured me. "But you have to admit that you had just as much fun calling me your boyfriend as I had warning that pompous ass away from you."

"Pompous ass." Thinking about how appropriate the insult was, considering his personality and the start of his surname, I giggled. "Now I'm never going to be able to see him without calling him that in my head."

We got to the SUV, he helped me into the

passenger seat. "Considering how it started, I'm happy that the night went so well for you."

My laughter dried up at the reminder of that threatening letter. "Yeah, I never would have guessed that I'd actually enjoy myself with how freaked out I am. It's a good thing you came to see me as soon as you got back in town. I don't know what I would have done without you."

"You won't have to find out."

I stared up at him as he stroked his thumb across my cheek. "It isn't as though you can stay by my side twenty-four seven until this is resolved."

"I can damn well do my best to do exactly that until my Monday morning run with the team," he insisted with a determined gleam in his green orbs. "Hopefully, we'll know by then who the fuck is messing with you."

I wasn't thrilled about going back to my apartment alone, but I still found myself saying, "I don't know. That's asking an awful lot of you."

"You're not asking. I'm offering," he corrected before shaking his head. "No, make that I'm insisting. I should've had you pack a bag before we left your place because you're staying with me tonight."

I scrunched my nose. "I'm not sure that's the best idea."

"Fine, then I'll stay with you."

"If you'd given me half a second to finish saying what I was thinking, that's exactly what I was going to suggest since I have a guest bedroom and I didn't notice one at your place." Spotting the gleam in his eyes, I wagged my finger and teased, "Just because everyone in there thinks we're boyfriend and girlfriend doesn't mean you're going to talk me into bed that easily."

"I'm not interested in easy, baby." He winked at me. "I'm a Navy SEAL. Doing things the hard way comes with the job."

I let out a heartfelt sigh as he shut my door and rounded the front of the SUV to climb into the driver's seat. Turning to him, I whispered, "Thank you."

After starting the engine and pulling out of the parking spot, he tugged my hand over the console so he could hold it while he drove. "There's no need to thank me. I'd do just about anything for you. This is nothing."

"I think we're going to need to agree to disagree again because what you're doing is a big deal to me."

He flashed me a grin as he turned onto the road. "I like how you're not afraid to use my words against me. Your sassy side is sexy as hell."

"Although redheads are supposed to be famous for their tempers, I don't think anyone has ever called me that before." I ducked my head, a lock of hair falling in front of my face to hide my blush. "Maybe you bring the sassy side out of me."

"That's fine by me." He squeezed my hand. "I don't want you to ever feel as though you have to hide anything when we're together. You're not going to scare me away. The more I learn about you, the more I like you."

"It's the same for me." Tucking my hair behind my ear, I peeked at him through my lashes. "I already thought you were pretty incredible for taking Paul to rehab when you didn't even know us, but you somehow keep getting better."

"Even when I threaten to kick someone's ass for hitting on you right in front of me?"

"Yes," I admitted with a soft laugh. "Just so long as I don't get fired for it, feel free to warn off whomever you'd like."

"Hooyah," he murmured.

When we reached his building, he led me up to his apartment again so he could pack a bag for the night. Only when he came back out of his bedroom, the duffel he had slung over his broad shoulder was fuller than I'd expected. "Don't tell me that you're a high-maintenance guy."

"Pardon?" he asked, his brows drawing together.

I jerked my chin toward his bag. "That's a lot of stuff for just one night."

"Like I said, I plan to stick close to you until my duties pull me away. And even then, I'm going to make sure you're safe."

Judging by the determination in his hard voice, the person who put that note on my car would soon regret it.

6

SILAS

When we returned to Phoebe's apartment, she seemed a little quieter than she had the rest of the night. As she unlocked the door, she kept peeking up at me through her lashes. It was adorable, and I couldn't help smiling, which seemed to fluster her, amusing me further.

Once it was open, I put my hand on her shoulder to stop her from walking in ahead of me. "Let me check things out first." Phoebe bit her bottom lip, then nodded as her eyes darted around nervously.

Inside, I dropped my bag on the floor before crossing the living room to check the sliding glass door that led out to her small balcony. It was still locked up tight, so I moved on to the kitchen, each bedroom, and the bathroom before returning to give her the all clear.

Phoebe walked in and shut the door, then bolted it. She set her purse on a little table in the entry, then kicked off her shoes.

"Would you like something to drink?" she asked as she wandered toward the kitchen.

"Sure, baby. Let me just drop my stuff in the bedroom."

She flashed a brief smile at me. "You can stay in Sage's old room, it's the first door on the right." Then she disappeared into the kitchen.

I picked up my duffel and retraced my steps down the hallway but moved right on past the first room and entered the second. Even though she'd warned me that she wouldn't easily fall into bed with me, I was amused that she thought I wouldn't be sleeping with her when her safety was at risk. She'd figure it out when we were ready to go to bed.

I looked around the decent-sized bedroom and noted that it had her personality splashed all over it. The art on the walls and the pillows on her bed were all bright colors and patterns. A fuzzy blanket was tossed over the end of the bed, and I could picture her curled up with it wrapped around her.

The only thing that gave me pause was the size

of her bed. It was only a double, and I mentally cringed thinking about trying to fit my tall, bulky frame into it. Then a smile played at the corners of my mouth as I thought, *I'll just have to wrap myself around my girl to conserve space.*

I ambled back out to the living room and into the kitchen. Phoebe was drinking from a bottle of water, and I stopped for a moment to admire the elegant slope of her neck as she tilted her head back. When she finished and lowered the bottle, her eyes meant mine. She must've seen some of the heat in my gaze because her cheeks dusted with a hint of pink.

"What would you like to drink?" she queried as she turned to open the refrigerator, then looked back at me. "I have some beer left over from the last time my dad was here."

"A beer would be great," I told her with a soft smile as I took a few steps forward to lessen the gap between us.

Phoebe turned to look inside, rustled around for a moment, then she backed away and closed the door with a swish of her hips because both her hands were full. She gave me a dark brown longneck bottle and set the wine in her other hand on the counter. Then she turned around to open another cabinet where there was a stash of glasses.

I almost laughed when she filled her glass to the brim, except that I knew her anxiety stemmed from fear, and I didn't like her being afraid.

However, while this wasn't what I would have chosen for the start of our relationship, I couldn't help but appreciate how fast the situation would get me into her bed. Which probably made me an asshole...but that wouldn't stop me from using this to my advantage. Even if nothing sexual happened between us for a while, I wanted to sleep with my arms wrapped around her.

I took a pull from my beer and once again admired her gorgeous body as she gulped down her drink. "Slow down baby," I urged her with a chuckle. She gave me a half smile and shrugged before taking a smaller sip. I cocked my head to the side and studied her for a moment, then asked, "Are you scared?"

Phoebe looked past my shoulder for a second before returning her gaze to my face and nibbling on her lip as she nodded. Then she sighed and admitted, "I feel much safer with you here."

I hastily closed the distance between us to take her glass so I could set both of our drinks on the counter. She watched me, her big blue eyes a mixture of curiosity and heat as I placed one hand on her waist and cupped the back of her head with the other. "I'm glad you feel safe with me. I won't let anything happen to you."

Phoebe leaned in and slipped her arms around my waist, resting her cheek against my chest.

She felt so damn good in my arms, all those soft curves pressed against me. A little voice in my head reminded me that I'd been very patient throughout the night and focused on her protection. I'd promised myself I could indulge once we were alone.

But was she ready for that?

I gently grasped the hair at the back of her head and drew it back, tilting her chin up so I could look directly into her beautiful face. We stared at each other in silence, both of us trying to figure out what came next. When Phoebe's eyelids began to droop, I gave in to my need and bent my head, sealing my mouth over hers.

Electricity zinged from our lips to every nerve ending in my body, lighting me up like a fucking Christmas tree. When a tiny moan escaped her mouth, I felt as if all the blood in my brain drained straight to my cock. Shifting the hand I had at her waist down to cup one of her round ass cheeks, my fingers flexed instinctively as I brought her even closer. She let out a little gasp when she felt the proof of my arousal pressed against her stomach, and I took full advantage, plunging my tongue into her sweet mouth. She tasted amazing, and I was instantly addicted.

Phoebe moved her hands to rest on my pecs, then she slid them up and locked them behind my neck. I groaned, and with a small tug of my hand, I tilted her head to change the angle of our kiss, deepening it.

It took a monumental effort to keep myself in control so that I wouldn't fuck her right there on the kitchen floor. After a few more minutes of devouring her lips, I forced myself to break away, although I didn't release her. She was blinking up at me, her eyes hazy with desire, and it nearly shredded my resolve.

"You taste even better than I imagined," I mumbled. "And trust me, I imagined a lot."

Phoebe's face was flushed from our kissing, but it didn't hide the pretty blush that bloomed on her cheeks.

"Me too," she whispered before nibbling on her bottom lip again. Instinctively, I lowered my head and used my teeth to pull her lip free, then nibbled the soft flesh briefly before releasing it.

"Only I get to bite these sexy lips," I told her sternly.

Phoebe's little pink tongue darted out and wet her lips, leaving them shiny—which introduced a whole new set of dirty images filling my mind.

I blinked them away and scanned her face, frowning at the purple smudges under her eyes. I should have been paying better attention because she was clearly exhausted.

"Are you ready for bed, baby?"

She mumbled an agreement, and I gave her another quick kiss on the forehead before releasing her. Patting her on the ass, I gently pushed her toward the door. "Go get ready. I just need to make a phone call."

I emptied her glass and the rest of my bottle into the sink, then threw the bottle into the recycle bin and put the glass in the dishwasher.

Once I finished cleaning up, I made a quick call to Deacon and filled him in on the night's events. I rummaged in the fridge while we talked and found sandwich fixings. He promised to look into it. After we hung up, I practically inhaled my sandwich, then I did one more round of all the doors and windows to make sure they were secure before I made my way to Phoebe's bedroom.

The door to the bathroom was closed, and there was no light shining beneath it, so I wasn't surprised to find the room empty. I made a beeline for my duffel bag and pulled out a pair of basketball shorts. Then I quickly took off my other clothes and put them on.

A minute later, I heard footsteps approaching the door, and Phoebe appeared. My eyes did a once-over from the top of her coppery curls to her cute, pink-tipped toes. Her hair floated down all around her shoulders, and her face was a little pink from being scrubbed clean. I took in her long T-shirt that made it look like she had nothing on underneath it and clenched my jaw. Half of me hoped that was the case, and the other side prayed she wore underwear. If not, I didn't think I'd be able to keep things rated PG tonight. When I returned my focus to her face, I smirked because her blue pools were glued to my chest and hazy with desire.

"I'm sorry," she sputtered suddenly, her feet shifting nervously beneath her. "I guess I wasn't clear enough. This is my room."

I raised an eyebrow and chuckled. "I'm a fucking Navy SEAL, baby. You really think I didn't figure that out?"

Phoebe's lips curled up, and her eyes twinkled with amusement, but she still looked adorably confused. "If you know this is my room, why are you in here?"

"Once again," I said with a long-suffering sigh, "I am reminding you of my promise not to leave your side." I wasn't sure if she noticed that this time, I left off the part about "until she was safe." I certainly wouldn't physically leave her until I knew that was the case, but I didn't want her to misunderstand either. This was not temporary. I wouldn't be letting her go. *Ever*.

"I know I mentioned that good girls get rewarded..." A wicked grin stole across my face. "With rewards come punishments."

Phoebe's mouth opened and formed an O that made my dick twitch. I was dying to feel those sexy lips wrapped around my shaft.

I let that hang in the air for a few heavy moments, then changed the subject. I didn't want to push her too hard, too fast.

"I don't want to be so far away from you if you need me."

A trickle of relief in her expression told me I wouldn't have to fight her on this. Then she nervously glanced between the bed and me.

"Um, I think I might have a sleeping bag. I'll go check."

Before she could take more than a couple of steps, I was across the room, grabbing her arm and swinging her around to wrap her up in my embrace.

"I'm not sleeping on the floor," I grunted.

Phoebe glanced at the bed again, then back at me. "I don't think you'll fit."

I laughed and gave her a hug before releasing her and patting her on the ass—thank fuck I felt a panty line—to get her moving toward the mattress. "We'll make it work, baby."

Phoebe slowly climbed under the covers, tossing skittish looks as I checked the windows and shut out the lights before walking to the other side of the bed. She had rolled onto her side, facing me, and watched as I joined her. To my surprise—and delight—when I lay on my back and held out my arm, she immediately scooted over and snuggled into my side.

She rested her head on my chest, and I began to run my fingers through her long, silky locks. After a beat, she fully relaxed, practically melting into me.

"Just to be clear, baby," I grunted.

Phoebe raised her head and met my gaze.

"I was serious about being close in order to protect you," I continued. "But I am not going to hide the fact that it's taking all of my energy not to fuck you right now. That doesn't mean you have anything to be afraid of with me. I promise nothing will happen between us until you're ready."

Her expression was soft as she smiled. "You can be awfully sweet, you know that?"

I scowled playfully and growled, "Navy SEALs aren't sweet, baby. We are motherfucking badasses."

Phoebe giggled. "Your secret is safe with me."

7

PHOEBE

Since I'd never spent the night with anyone before, I'd expected to have difficulty drifting off last night, especially since my bed wasn't exactly made for two people when one of us was as big as Silas. But with his arms wrapped around me, I had never slept better.

Waking up to find him stretched out beneath me was the best, though. He was gorgeous when he was awake, but he was even more so with his face relaxed and his plump lips slightly open as puffs of air escaped. Something about him commanded attention from everyone around him, but I felt the pull to him even more strongly seeing him vulnerable like this.

I couldn't resist the temptation to brush my lips

against his bristly jaw, and Silas went from sound asleep to wide awake in the blink of an eye. Alertness flared in his eyes as he stared up at me, then a smile curved his lips. "Morning, baby. Did you sleep okay?"

"Uh-huh." I sat up, and my cheeks heated at being caught ogling him while he wasn't aware. "You?"

He curled up, his abs clenching into more of an eight-pack than a six. "Yup, I think I found my new favorite blanket."

"You did?" My brows drew together as I glanced down at my lavender comforter. "It isn't too girly for you?"

His hands gripped my hips, and he pulled me against his chest. "I was talking about you, baby. You spent most of the night sprawled on top of me."

"Oh, sorry about that." My cheeks heated more.

"No need to apologize. You can do it again whenever you want, and you won't get any complaints from me. It was fucking fantastic," he reassured me, swiping his thumb against my bottom lip. "And waking up to your gorgeous face is already a great start to my morning."

"I was thinking the same." His stomach let out a growl. "But I'm willing to bet that a big breakfast will make it even better since you barely ate anything last night."

"I could definitely eat," he confirmed.

I slid off the mattress and asked, "Do you only eat healthy stuff like boring egg whites and fruit in the morning, or would you like some of my famous cream cheese-stuffed French toast topped with strawberries and whipped cream?"

"When you put it that way, I'm gonna have to go with the second option." He patted his abs with a grin. "Today would've been a cheat day for me anyway."

"That's a lucky thing because it would've sucked for you to have to eat an uber healthy breakfast while I stuffed my face with delicious French toast."

"But I'm hungry for something else first," he muttered as he crawled off the mattress to stand in front of me. Cupping the back of my head, he pulled me close and lowered his head to capture my lips.

I didn't have time to worry about my morning breath as his tongue swept inside my mouth. The kiss he gave me last night had been amazing, but this one was even better. It was deep, wet, and demanding. All I could do was clutch his shoulders as I lost myself in his kiss.

When he finally lifted his head again, I let out a

soft whimper because I wasn't ready for it to be over. "Don't worry, baby. There are plenty more of those in your future."

"Wow," I breathed, pressing my fingers against my tingling lips. "Now that's a great way to start my morning."

"Damn straight." He brushed his mouth against mine, then turned me to face the door. With a gentle swat on my butt, he murmured, "You better get moving if we're going to have any hope of making it out of this room today."

I was tempted to take him up on the sensual promise in his deep voice, but his stomach rumbled again. Figuring that I owed him a good meal, at the very least, with everything he was doing for me, I flashed him a smile over my shoulder. "It'll take me about forty-five minutes to make breakfast. Would you like some coffee while you wait?"

"I'd love some," he agreed with a smile. "But would you mind if I use your shower first?"

"Not at all."

I headed into the kitchen, but my mind stayed with Silas in my bathroom. It was too easy to picture him naked with hot water pounding against his muscular, broad back. Focusing on prepping all the ingredients for my French toast wasn't easy, but I had the sweet cream filling in the fridge to cool and everything else out and ready to go by the time he joined me in the kitchen.

Jerking my chin toward the end of the counter, I murmured, "Coffee's ready if you want to grab a cup. Do you want some flavored creamer or sugar?"

"I take mine black," he replied as he poured coffee into the mug that I'd left out for him.

I leaned into the fridge to pull out the bowl of filling. "I should've guessed since you're a big, tough SEAL."

"Nah." He shook his head and took a sip. "There's nothing unmanly about cream or sugar. A few of the guys on the team take theirs that way."

I quirked a brow. "And is it safe to say you like to tease them about it?"

"Yeah, we do," he confirmed with a chuckle. "Anything I can help you with?"

"Nope, I have it under control."

I proved that true fifteen minutes later when I slid a plate in front of him before grabbing mine to join him at the table. Silas hummed in pleasure as he dug into his breakfast, making the extra effort more than worthwhile. Once we finished, he insisted on cleaning up while I showered.

I had never been happier to have a weekend

without any plans because I got to spend all day with Silas. We didn't even do anything special, just watched some shows cuddled on my couch in the living room. Since we were both full from breakfast, we skipped lunch and just ordered pizza for dinner later.

We had so much fun. Time seemed to fly by, and it was already eight o'clock when I got a call. Reluctantly pulling away from Silas, I reached toward the coffee table to grab my phone. My brows drew together when I glanced at the screen and didn't recognize the number.

"What's wrong?" Silas asked, sitting up to look at the screen as well.

"Nothing, really. I just don't know who's calling." I pressed my lips together. "But it's a local area code, so maybe it's Paul using a phone at the rehab center?"

His eyes were concerned as he shrugged. "You should take it, just in case. But would you mind putting the call on speaker mode when you answer? If it's your brother, I'll give you some privacy to chat with him."

I nodded, doing as he requested before I said, "Hello?"

"I warned you," a voice hissed. With the low

pitch and robotic sound, the caller was obviously using a voice distorter.

"Who is this?" I cried, looking up at Silas in dismay while I felt grateful that he could hear what was being said.

"The person you should be listening to if you know what's good for you."

I gripped Silas's hand and held on for dear life as my entire body trembled. "Did you leave a note on my car yesterday?"

"Yes, but I wanted to make sure you understood since it's all your fault!"

I shook my head, my brows drawing together as tears filled my eyes. "I don't understand. What's all my fault?"

"The guy you were with yesterday might have fallen for your dumb redhead act, but not me. If I can't be happy, then you shouldn't either. It isn't fair when you've ruined everything!"

The caller hadn't just put the note on my car and left. They must have stuck around and seen me with Silas. Thank goodness he hadn't let me go to my event alone. Something horrible could've happened to me if I'd been on my own.

I had no idea what the caller was talking about, but that didn't stop me from apologizing in the hopes that it would deescalate the situation. "I'm sorry if I've done something to hurt you. I swear I didn't mean to."

"Empty words mean nothing, but you'll know the true meaning of being sorry soon enough."

My heart was beating so fast, it felt as though it was going to burst through my chest. The note had been scary enough, but knowing this person had somehow gotten my phone number so they could call and terrorize me took the situation to a whole new level. Even with Silas's strong presence at my side, I was terrified.

8

SILAS

Phoebe's phone slipped from her hand, but thanks to my quick reflexes, I caught the device before it hit the ground. I set it on the coffee table and pulled Phoebe into my body, wrapping my arms around her.

"I don't understand why this is happening to me," she said, her voice trembling.

"I don't know, baby, but I promise I'll keep you safe."

She was staring off into the distance, not really looking at anything, but my words seemed to snap her out of it. Her eyes came to meet mine, and the terror I saw in them was killing me. A tear trickled down her cheek, and I quickly swiped it away with my thumb, but it was just the start. I cradled her head against my chest as she quietly cried and dug my cell phone out of my pocket with my other hand. I hit Deacon's number and put the phone to my ear as it started ringing.

He picked up after two rings.

"Hey, Silas, I was going to call you in a couple of hours. There was a partial print on the note, but not enough for us to get a hit in any database. So I sent it to a friend who works with a specialist who might be able to reconstruct it enough for us to at least narrow the options down to a handful of people. Of course, that's assuming they're in any system."

I squeezed my eyes shut, frustrated that this wasn't falling into place as quickly as I wanted. "Phoebe just got a threatening phone call," I informed him. He practically interrogated me for the next few minutes, but I didn't mind because I knew he was just trying to be thorough. If it were his wife, I would do the same for him.

Phoebe calmed down shortly after I started the call, so I put Deacon on speaker, and she was able to answer some of his questions better than I could.

"I'll get to working on the trace," Deacon promised when we finished. "If she kept them on the line long enough, we might be able to get a hit on a location. We'll go from there."

"Thank you," I replied before ending the call and putting my phone on the table next to Phoebe's.

I wrapped her up in my arms again and placed a soft kiss on her forehead before whispering. "We're going to figure this out, baby."

Phoebe swallowed hard, but I could see the trust in her gaze when she nodded.

"How about you go take a bath while I make you some hot tea?" I suggested. I'd seen all of the girly shit in the bathroom, especially around the tub, and figured a bath would relax her.

One corner of Phoebe's mouth lifted. "How did you know I love baths?"

I rolled my eyes playfully and jabbed my chest with my thumb. "Navy SEAL, remember?"

This time, Phoebe gave me a real smile. "Right, how could I forget? A motherfucking badass."

A laugh burst from my chest, and I hugged her close. "You're adorable, Phoebe Baker." When my laughter faded, I put my finger under her chin and raised her face so she could see my expression and know that I was completely serious. "But don't say shit like that in front of other people, or I'll have to spank your ass. Don't get me wrong, the idea of filthy words coming out of your sweet mouth is hot as hell, but only for me. Is that clear?"

Phoebe looked around, then back up at me. "But we are alone," she stated cheekily.

A smile spread across my face, and I winked at her. "Exactly, baby. And that's why you're not getting a spanking this time."

Phoebe bit her lip but released it when I growled and smirked at me instead. She untangled herself from my embrace and walked toward the hallway, but she stopped at the entrance to look back at me over her shoulder with a saucy grin. "Too bad," she quipped before disappearing down the hall. I was too stunned to do anything before I heard the bathroom door click shut.

Fuck. I had seen glimpses of her sass over the past couple of days, but I couldn't wait to see her personality come out in full force. I was tempted to barge into the bathroom and join her in the tub, but it had been an emotional night, and I didn't want to take advantage of her fragile state. So I reluctantly went into the kitchen and put a kettle of water on the stove.

When I heard the tub begin to drain, I flipped on the burner to warm the water. I'd just finished removing the tea bag from her mug when I heard the slap of bare feet on the linoleum, and Phoebe entered the kitchen.

I about swallowed my tongue when I looked up and saw her in a purple tank top and matching sleep shorts. The material wasn't thin enough for me to see if she was wearing underwear, but it couldn't hide the hard nipples on her big tits. "Stand down," I silently ordered my dick. But it didn't give a shit what my brain wanted.

I gestured toward the table and croaked, "Tea."

Phoebe's answering smile made her look wholesome with her damp hair curling around her makeup-free face, bringing out the sprinkle of freckles across her nose and cheeks.

If I were a better man, I might have stopped to consider whether I should be corrupting this sweet thing. But I wasn't, and I was very much looking forward to showing her how good it felt to be dirty.

"I'm gonna go hop in the shower," I rasped before making a hasty exit.

I'd already taken one this morning, but the frigid shower managed to calm my libido down a little bit. It was the best I could hope for because when it came to Phoebe, I was always sporting at least a semi.

I dried off and pulled on my basketball shorts, brushed my teeth, and trimmed my facial hair. When those things were done, I stared at myself in the mirror and frowned. I was procrastinating, and I knew it. I was hoping she'd be asleep by the time I got into bed. Her fear had magnified all the protective and possessive feelings coursing through me, leaving me on edge. Which made it harder to control my growing need for her.

I quietly opened the bathroom door and padded silently down the hall, just in case she was asleep. Luck had clearly abandoned me, because I heard the low hum of the television in the living room.

I headed that way and spotted Phoebe curled up on the couch with the blanket from the end of her bed wrapped around her. She stared blankly at the wall above the television with her mug of tea cradled in her hands.

I walked over and gently removed the cup, then set it on the table.

"Let's get you to bed, baby." She blinked a few times before looking up at me. I would be even happier when all of this was over just so I could see Phoebe's beautiful face without the tiredness lurking in her blue depths and the shadows under her eyes.

When she didn't make a move to get up, I scooped her into my arms and carried her back to the bedroom. I pulled the comforter back with one hand, then gently set her down on the mattress before covering her with the blanket.

I took a few steps toward the door, but the sound of her frantic voice calling my name brought me to a quick halt. I spun around to see her watching me with those beautiful eyes once again brimming with tears.

"You're not going to stay with me?"

I arched my brow and stared at her until the corners of her lips lifted, and she nodded. "Not leaving my side. Right. How could I forget?" Relief trickled through me when she giggled.

I'd been hoping for that reaction, and I was pleased to see a little of the fear and tiredness slip away.

"I'm just going to do a once-over, and make sure the alarm is set, then I'll be back."

"Okay," she whispered with a sweet smile as she scooted back down to lay on her back.

Once I made sure everything was secure, I returned to the bedroom to find that she had fallen asleep. I shut off the light and slipped into the bed next to her before gently curling my body around hers.

THE SOUND of quiet crying jerked me out of a deep sleep.

My eyes flew open, and I jackknifed up in bed, looking around wildly for the threat. When I didn't see anything, I turned to look down at Phoebe and realized she was asleep. I felt a stab in my heart at the wetness shimmering on her cheeks. She was having a bad dream.

Gently, I tapped her cheek, then ran my hand over her head and down the side of her face. "Baby, wake up," I called softly. "You're having a bad dream, Phoebe. Come on, baby, wake up for me."

Finally, Phoebe came awake with a jolt and sat up, looking around with wild blue eyes until she figured out where she was and who she was with. As soon as her gaze landed on me, she threw herself into my arms and climbed onto my lap. She straddled me with her legs curled around my hips, and her arms went around my torso, squeezing so hard I was a little worried she might crack a rib. I kept one arm banded securely around her and smoothed my other hand over her hair and down her back, repeatedly. "I'm here. You're safe. I won't let anything happen to you."

I kept whispering reassuring words in her ear and soothing her with my touch until her trembles finally subsided. Her face was buried in my neck, and I tried to ignore the feel of her hot breath on the sensitive skin. I didn't need to be any harder than I already was.

"Are you all right?" I inquired gently.

Phoebe raised her head, and as I tried to read the tumultuous emotions in her stormy blue eyes, I was taken aback by the heat in them.

"No," she muttered with a sharp shake of her head.

"What do you need, baby?"

Phoebe licked her lips and swallowed as her eyes dropped to my mouth, then traveled back up to meet my gaze. "I need you to kiss me."

It probably made me an even bigger asshole for not questioning her demand. She was scared and emotionally vulnerable. A better man wouldn't take advantage of that. Clearly, I wasn't one because her request snapped in my control.

My fingers dove into her hair, and I twisted it around my fist so I could tug her head back and crash my mouth down onto hers.

9

PHOEBE

My dream was beyond horrible, but as soon as I looked into Silas's eyes and realized it wasn't real, I knew I was okay. Only because he was there and wouldn't have it any other way. Knowing this, any doubts I had about my readiness to sleep with him disappeared.

His kiss was exactly what I needed to forget all the bad and only focus on the good. To anchor me in the tumultuous sea I'd been unwillingly tossed into by the person who wanted to hurt me.

I hadn't counted on how quickly our kiss would spiral out of control, but I would have happily lost myself in it for hours. So when Silas tore his mouth from mine with a groan and dropped his head back against the pillow, I didn't let him get far. "I want more."

"More what, baby?"

His dick was hard beneath me, and I rolled my hips to slide against him. "Anything and everything you want to give me."

"Fuuuck," he groaned, his hold on my hair tightening. "Are you sure? I don't want to take advantage of you being vulnerable. We have all the time in the world for sex since you won't be able to get rid of me."

I brushed my lips against his and whispered, "I have no plans of trying to get rid of you, and I don't want to wait. I'm more than ready for this."

My answer must have been what he was waiting for because he flipped our positions so fast, it made my head spin. When I was flat on my back with his body pressed against mine, he captured my mouth in another deep kiss that left me breathless. I didn't have the chance to protest when he ended it this time because I was too busy turning my head to give him better access to my neck as he trailed his lips down to my pulse point.

His hands drifted down my sides to grip the hem of my tank top, and I lifted off the mattress so he could tug the soft cotton material up and over my head. I hadn't bothered with a bra since we were headed to bed after my bath, and my nipples pebbled beneath his heated gaze.

"So fucking perfect," he rasped, lowering his head to suck one of my puckered peaks into his mouth.

I threaded my fingers through his hair to press him closer to my chest as I moaned, "Oh yes."

He let my nipple go with a pop and looked up at me. "You like that, baby?"

I nodded. "So much."

"Good." He gave the other side the same treatment before adding, "I'll want to spend a lot of time playing with your perfect tits, but right now, I need to get a taste of your pussy."

My inner walls fluttered at his words, and I lifted my hips off the mattress so he could tug my sleep shorts down my legs. His gaze heated as he stared down at me. "Such a pretty pussy. I can't wait to get my mouth on you. Part your legs even more for me, baby."

I was completely bared to his sight, and my blush swept from my cheeks across my chest as I slowly moved my legs wider. I was incredibly turned on already, and I felt my wetness dripping from my core.

"That's my good girl." Licking his lips, Silas trailed his finger over my freckles in the valley between my breasts. "It shouldn't be possible for you to be so damn cute and sexy at the same time."

"Silas, please," I whimpered.

His eyes locked on mine. "You deserve a reward for being so courageous, don't you?"

I nodded. "Uh-huh."

"We'll both be rewarded." He pressed his chest against the mattress and wedged his shoulders between my thighs. "You'll get an orgasm, and I'll finally have the taste of your sweet pussy filling my mouth."

The air caught in my lungs as he lowered his head, his breath hot against my core. Inhaling deeply, he groaned before closing the gap between us. Then he drew his tongue up my slit, from bottom to top. The pleasure was so overwhelming, I jerked away from him with a gasp. "Whoa."

Glancing up at me with heated eyes, he asked, "Are you ready for more?"

"Yes, please," I whispered.

His gaze lowered again, and he used his thumbs to pull back my folds. "So fucking drenched for me," he muttered, his voice full of masculine appreciation.

My clit was practically throbbing with need, and

when he ran the tip of his tongue around it and over the top, I felt the zing of pleasure deep inside me.

"Oh, my gosh," I gasped, going up on my elbows so I could watch him go down on me. His eyes were zeroed in on my pussy as he licked up my wetness. Then he stiffened his tongue and stabbed it inside my entrance, and my entire body grew taut. "I'm close already, Silas."

"Good, baby. Come for me," he commanded. "I want to hear your cries echo off the walls while your pussy strangles my tongue."

The combination of his dirty words and his tongue working me right after was enough to send me over the edge. I cried out and my body shuddered, my inner walls clamping down on his tongue just like he'd wanted. He licked me through my orgasm, not letting up until my body stopped trembling.

"Good girl." He kissed the inside of my thigh. "Now I want to feel you come around my fingers. Need to make sure you're ready to get off when my cock stretches your perfect pussy."

I'd only ever orgasmed on my own before, and the one he'd just given me was more powerful than anything I'd experienced. But it didn't prepare me for what it would feel like when Silas started to work one of his thick fingers inside me inch by inch. "So damn tight."

"Um, yeah...about that," I whispered, realizing I hadn't shared my lack of experience with him and hoping it wouldn't make a difference.

His digit slid a little deeper as his gaze drifted up my body to scan my face. "What, baby? No need to be nervous, you can tell me anything."

"I've never done this before."

His body went rock solid, the green of his eyes deepening. "I'm the first man to get a taste of you?"

"Uh-huh." I nodded and let out a nervous breath. "The first for any of this, actually."

"That's my good girl, saving herself for me." He sank his finger farther inside my tight channel. "I swear I'm going to make this good for you, baby. I'll never give you a reason to regret waiting until I found you."

"You're not mad?" I asked, butterflies swirling in my belly over his reaction.

"Not even a little bit," he assured me with a smug grin. "I'm fucking thrilled that I'm the only man who'll ever get to see you like this. I love that you'll only ever be mine."

I knew that people said things in the heat of the moment, but his possessive words made my heart swell. They also amped up my desire, which he took full advantage of by twisting his wrist. The pad of his finger stroked against the sensitive spot inside, and he lowered his head to flick his tongue over my clit before tugging it between his teeth.

Fireworks exploded behind my eyelids as waves of pleasure crashed over my body. "Silas, yes! Oh yes!"

He worked me through my second release, and then he got to his knees and shoved his basketball shorts down his thick thighs. After he tossed them over his shoulder, he wrapped my legs around his waist and notched the tip of his dick at my entrance. When his gaze met mine, he asked, "Ready, baby?"

"Absolutely."

As the last syllable of my reply trailed off, he thrust forward in one powerful shift of his hips, filling me completely. He hadn't given me the chance to tense before pushing through my innocence, and the pain didn't hit me until his balls had already slapped against my butt.

Bending low, Silas kissed the tears from my cheeks and murmured, "I'm sorry, baby. Shh, don't cry. It'll pass soon, and then I'll give you more plea-sure than you can stand for being such a good girl."

He kissed me until the ache eased, and I wiggled my hips experimentally. "It's better now."

"Thank fuck," he groaned. "Being inside you without moving is the best kind of torture."

He pulled his hips back before thrusting all the way in again. Throwing his head back, he growled, "Fuck, yes! You're so damn tight, baby. Not sure how long I'm going to be able to last."

Digging my heels into his butt, I urged Silas on, desperate to see him lose control. "Don't hold back. I need you."

His pace started to pick up until he was hammering me into the mattress over and over again. "You're doing so good, baby. Taking every fucking inch of my cock your first time. More proof that you were made for me, just like I thought."

He slid his hands under my butt and lifted me toward him on the next thrust, circling his hips to grind against my clit. My pussy clamped down hard around his dick, and I started to come again. "Yes! Oh, yes!"

"That's it, Phoebe. Milk my come from my cock and take it all," he grunted as his hard shaft twitched. Then he slammed deep, holding still with his dick anchored deep inside me while we came together.

It wasn't until the shudders subsided and I

caught my breath that I finally realized Silas had taken me bare. My head jerked back so I could stare at him with wide eyes as I gasped, "Crap, we didn't use a condom."

"I know, baby. But that's okay because whatever happens, you're mine."

10

SILAS

I growled in annoyance at the sound of my phone ringing. Burying my face in the crook of Phoebe's neck, I tightened my arms around her as I brought her naked body closer to mine.

I was going to let it go to voicemail when it occurred to me that the caller might have news on Phoebe's stalker. Grunting in frustration, I reluctantly released her and rolled over to grab my cell off the nightstand.

Without looking at the caller ID, I swiped to answer and put the phone to my ear. "This better be fucking good," I snapped.

Deacon snickered, "Did I disturb your dirty dreams about your girl?"

"Worse, asshole," I snarled. "The real thing."

Deacon laughed. "Wow, you didn't waste any time, did you?"

I rolled my eyes even though he couldn't see it. "You're one to talk."

"That's fair," Deacon admitted with another chuckle.

"Did you call just to be an ass or do you have actual information for me?" I muttered.

Phoebe's head popped up, and she twisted around to look at me over her shoulder. I mouthed, "Deacon," and she immediately rolled over and sat up. I averted my eyes from her gorgeous breasts as the sheet fell to her waist. *Now is not the time, Atwood.*

"I'm sure you already guessed that the phone was a burner," he started.

"Shit." He was right. I wasn't surprised, but that didn't mean I wasn't irritated as shit.

"Don't get your panties in a twist just yet," he continued. "We got a ping on the location where it was used and went to check it out. At the time of the call, it was at or near a diner one town over from Phoebe's apartment. I acquired the footage, and I'm emailing it to you now."

"Since you haven't given me a name, I assume it doesn't reveal the identity of the bastard?"

"No, but there were a few people on cell phones within the radius of the camera at the right time. The place's security is shit, but I wondered if Phoebe might recognize someone even though the images are pretty pixelated."

"I'll have her take a look and get back to you," I replied.

"Hooyah," Deacon granted before ending the call.

I'd scooted up to lean against the headboard, and when I set down my phone, Phoebe crawled up to sit next to me. Slipping my arm around her, I explained, "Deacon has some footage he wants you to look at. I don't know if it will give us anything, but I think it's worth a try."

Phoebe's expression turned hopeful, and she nodded. "Sure. Do you have it?"

I grabbed her around the waist with my other arm and dragged her onto my lap so she was straddling me. "Good morning," I murmured.

Phoebe canted her head to the side and repeated, "Good morning."

I crooked my finger, and she leaned in. Then I grabbed her chin between my fingers and captured her mouth in a deep kiss. When I let her up for air, she was flushed and dazed, making me grin.

"That's how we start our mornings, baby. I don't care what the fuck is happening around us."

Her lips formed a dreamy smile, and her cheeks were painted pink. "I can get on board with that," she sighed happily.

I jerked my chin to the left, indicating the little desk where I'd left my computer. "I'll grab my laptop, and we can look at the footage."

As she moved off my lap, my attention was stolen by the sway of her heavy tits, but I forced myself to focus on the situation at hand. I could feast on those later.

I padded over to the desk and picked up the computer. Then I looked around the floor until I spotted her tank top and quickly picked it up. I tossed it to her as I headed back to the bed. She caught it easily and raised her brow in question.

I dropped my eyes to her chest, and then back up to her face, and mumbled, "You're too tempting, I can't focus."

Phoebe blushed hard, but her expression was filled with pleasure as she shot me a wicked smile before donning the shirt. Then she glanced pointedly at my cock, which was standing straight up and bounced against my stomach with each step. "That goes both ways, sailor."

I laughed, but instead of finding my shorts, I winked and crawled back onto the mattress. Once I was sitting against the headboard again, I flung the sheet over my lap.

Phoebe snorted and shook her head. "Cheater."

I smiled devilishly. "Easy access, baby."

Phoebe giggled, but her amusement faded away as I lifted the lid of my laptop.

She scooted up to my side so she could see the screen as it woke up, and I clicked the envelope icon to open my email. Deacon's message was there, and I downloaded the attachment. Before opening it, I looked at Phoebe and asked softly, "Are you sure you're okay to look at this?"

"Yeah. It's just people on the phone, right?"

"True. Still, I don't like anything upsetting you."

"Well," she said with a shrug, "we don't really have a choice if we want this to stop, do we?"

I frowned, knowing she was right, but still not happy about it.

The footage was only about two minutes long since the call had been barely thirty seconds. But it was enough time to see what direction the callers came from and then went.

The video showed a twenty-four-hour greasy spoon, most of the parking lot, and the sidewalks on either side that divided it from the other buildings surrounding the place.

Phoebe stared intently at the screen as she scrutinized each person who walked into the camera's view, but as the video neared the end, she began to look discouraged. "I don't see anyone who—"

She stopped suddenly and leaned forward so her nose was nearly touching the screen. A hooded figure had exited the diner and was standing just to the right of the door making a call.

"Is that a woman?"

I paused the video and zoomed in. "That would be my assessment," I confirmed. "Good eye, baby."

She stared at the screen in thoughtful silence for a few moments, then mumbled, "Something about her is familiar."

Even without Phoebe's comment, I knew in my gut that this woman was the one we were looking for. Unfortunately, there wasn't anything distinguishing that would help us find her.

When the unknown woman finished her call, she walked into the parking lot. I held my breath, hoping we'd be able to see whatever car she drove off in. Even though my rational mind knew that if he'd seen the vehicle, Deacon would have been all over it by now.

In the next frame, the figure's hood was blown back by a gust of wind. She caught it as it fell and pulled it back up. But the material was down long enough to give us a split-second view of her face.

"Play that part again," Phoebe requested.

I did as she asked, and we both watched it carefully one more time.

Phoebe put a finger to her lips and tapped as she contemplated the video.

"Do you recognize her?" I asked.

She raised discouraged eyes to my face and shook her head. "No, but something about her is just so familiar. I can't put my finger on it."

I closed the laptop and set it on the other side of the bed. Then I pulled Phoebe onto my lap and wrapped my arms around her. She leaned into my embrace, resting her head on my shoulder.

"We'll figure this out," I promised. "I want to try something with you. Let's call Deacon in a bit, and you can describe the video to him."

Phoebe lifted her head and frowned at me. "He's already watched it, hasn't he? So what good would that do?"

"You'd be surprised what will come out of your mouth once you start talking. Our minds have an amazing capacity for recall, we just don't always know how to access it."

Phoebe tilted her head to the side and observed me with a sweet smile. "You're pretty amazing, you know that?" Then she smirked and teased, "Such a sweet guy."

I growled, and in seconds, I had her flipped on her back, her tank top off, and my body covering her from head to toe.

"I'll show you sweet," I muttered.

She giggled, but her laughter faded into a moan when my lips wrapped around one of her big, delicious nipples.

Over an hour later, I carried a very satisfied, boneless Phoebe into the bathroom so we could take a quick shower. Once we were dressed, we made our way to the kitchen, and while Phoebe puttered around looking for something to make for breakfast, I put a call into Deacon.

"Does she know who it is?" Deacon asked as soon as he picked up the phone.

"No, but the hooded figure at the diner entrance looks familiar to her. I'm going to have her describe the scene to you, and maybe you'll be able to pick up on any details that she recalls by trying to remember it."

"Good idea," Deacon replied.

"Baby," I called to Phoebe. I motioned for her to join me at the kitchen table. When she neared, I grasped her hips and pulled her down onto my lap. "I want you to close your eyes and think back over those seconds in the footage. Then try to describe what you were looking at to Deacon."

"Describe the person?" she asked dubiously.

"Everything. Anything you noticed. Other people, cars, colors, signs, anything."

Her nod was hesitant, but she obediently closed her eyes and began to talk.

I was impressed with the amount of detail she was able to recall.

When she finished, I smiled at her encouragingly. "That was fantastic, baby."

"I think you may have noticed a few things that we didn't," Deacon added. "Impressive, Phoebe."

She beamed at me, and lost in her smile, I mumbled, "Thanks, Deacon. Let me know what you find out."

After hanging up, I shifted Phoebe so she was sitting with her legs hanging on either side of mine. "I'm proud of you."

She sniffed haughtily. "I am good, aren't I?"

Laughter bubbled in my chest, and I bent my head to give her a long, deep kiss.

"I better feed you," I muttered against her lips. "Then I'm going to have you for lunch."

Phoebe giggled. "I don't think that will satisfy you."

"Challenge accepted. Hooyah."

11

PHOEBE

I had been racking my brain for the past day, trying to remember where I'd seen the woman in the video. Unfortunately, I just couldn't place her, no matter how much I tried. I had really been hoping that we'd be able to identify her before this morning so I wouldn't have to be afraid anymore.

I was supposed to be at the office in a couple of hours, but Silas had talked me into taking a sick day since my paid time off had already kicked in at work. I'd been nervous to call in, but my boss was sweet and just told me not to worry about it and to take care of myself.

Unfortunately, Silas couldn't play hooky from the base with me no matter how much I wished he could. The schedule of a Navy SEAL was much stricter than a marketing assistant in the hospitality industry.

Curled around my pillow on my bed, I pouted up at him as he pulled on a pair of workout shorts. "Are you sure you have to go?"

"Sorry, baby." He flashed me a sexy grin and padded over to the side of the bed. Pressing his palms into the mattress, he leaned over to give me a quick kiss. "I have to go in for morning PT, but I won't be gone too long. And it'll allow me to brainstorm this situation with the team. Maybe one of the guys will have an idea how to find this bitch."

"Okay," I huffed, burying my face in my pillow with a sigh.

"I really like the idea of you waiting in bed for me. I bet I'll be the first to finish our run today with motivation like that," he boasted.

Twisting my neck, I looked up at him and giggled. "If that means you'll get back faster, then you'd better be."

He snapped to attention and saluted me. "Yes, ma'am."

"As long as you're taking orders, I could use a cup of coffee before you go."

I was only teasing, but I shouldn't have been

surprised when he returned to my bedroom five minutes later with a steaming mug. "Here you go, baby. I went heavy on the flavored creamer, just how you like it."

Sitting up and reaching out to accept the coffee, I beamed him a smile. "You really didn't have to do this, but thank you."

"My pleasure."

I wagged my brows at him. "I'm hoping it will be both of ours when you come back."

He tugged a T-shirt over his head and smirked back at me. "Stay right there like a good girl, and it definitely will be."

"I promise, I'm not going anywhere." We'd stayed in the bubble of my apartment all weekend, and it had become my safe space...especially with Silas here. Without him at my side, I had no interest in running any of the errands I'd been putting off.

After he put on his socks and shoes, he gave me another kiss. I let out a dreamy sigh as I stared at his butt while he walked out of my bedroom.

I was super comfy in bed and could use some more rest since it was early. I hadn't slept much last night because Silas woke me twice to make love. So I heaved a deep sigh and grumbled to myself when there was a knock on the door only a few minutes after Silas left. "I wonder what he forgot?"

Setting my coffee on the bedside table, I crawled off the mattress and threw on my robe before stomping through my apartment. When I flung the door open, I got a big, unpleasant surprise.

I must have been more tired than I thought because I should have known Silas wouldn't have knocked if he'd left something behind. He had to have taken my keys so he could lock the door behind him, and he wouldn't have left me alone in bed when someone could walk right into my apartment without me being aware. Not when he'd kept it locked the entire time he'd been here to protect me.

Now he was gone, and I was facing off against the mysterious woman who'd threatened me all by myself. She wore the same hoodie from the video and clenched a big knife in her fist.

Holding my hands up in a gesture of surrender, I murmured, "Please don't hurt me."

"Get inside," she growled, shoving my shoulder with her free hand.

It wasn't until she kicked the door shut behind her that the hood fell back and I got my first glimpse of her face. Gasping, I pressed my hand against my chest. "I know you. I don't know your name, but we met at the rehab center. You were discharged when I went to visit my brother."

"Of course you don't know my name!" she shrieked, laughing maniacally. "Why would you bother to do something as basic as that before you destroyed my life?"

Between her pale skin, stringy hair, and dilated eyes, I was pretty sure she'd already fallen off the wagon and straight into a pile of whatever she was addicted to. I knew from experience that trying to argue logic with someone when they were high wouldn't work, but I had to at least try. "I'm sorry. Will you please tell me your name now? And what I did to hurt you?"

"I told you not to bother playing dumb." She took a menacing step toward me, jabbing the knife in my direction. "It's not going to work on me. Paul said I was smart. He did."

Her eyes lit up when she said my brother's name, the same way they had when she'd talked about him in the lobby of the rehab center. "My brother is a very good judge of character."

"He is," she agreed with a frantic nod. "And he likes me."

"I'm sure he does."

Her eyes narrowed, and her lips pressed

together. "Or at least he liked me when we could talk to each other. But you're ruining everything because you won't let him anymore."

"I don't control who my brother gets to talk to while he's at the rehab clinic," I pointed out in a soft voice. "You were a patient there. You know that's not how it works. The counselors decide how much contact it's safe for the patients to have, depending on where they are in their journey to becoming sober. Paul is still only allowed to talk to family, but that should change sometime this month."

"No," she hissed, shaking her head. "You went there, and I didn't get to talk to him again. It's because of you. It has to be. Paul wouldn't tell them that I couldn't call. You did. You even said so."

My brows drew together. "What did I say?"

"That the universe didn't want us to be together," she spat.

"Oh." I remembered saying something similar, but I hadn't thought for a moment that she would take it as me preventing her from having contact with Paul. "I didn't mean you specifically. I only meant that there are rules about not starting a new romantic relationship so soon after finishing rehab. Remember, I also said you might meet in the future...when you're both on solid ground and ready for more than friendship."

"No, no, no, no, no!" she screamed, pacing back and forth in front of me as she waved her hands in the air, the knife gleaming in the sunlight streaming through the window. "You told them to block my calls, I know you did."

"How would I do that? I don't even know your name," I reminded her.

Her eyes widened, and for a moment, I thought I had gotten through to her. Then her lip curled up in a snarl as she glared at me and closed the small distance between us. Her breath was hot on my face when she roared, "Stop trying to mess with my head! I warned you not to come between Paul and me, but you didn't listen. You could've called the center and told them to let me talk to him, but they still wouldn't let me through last night. Because you don't want us to be happy together. You want us to grow apart while he's stuck in that place for another month."

"I wouldn't do that to my brother," I denied with a shake of my head. "All I've ever wanted was for him to be happy."

"You're lying." She pressed the tip of the blade against my side. "If you were a good sister, he wouldn't have needed to convince you to visit him there. You would have wanted to see him like I do. But that's okay because Paul won't need to worry about having your negative influence in his life anymore. And we will be able to reunite soon...at your funeral."

12

SILAS

It was all I could do to force myself to leave Phoebe in that bed looking so sleepy and fuckable. I hadn't been kidding when I told her that I would bust my ass to get through the PT as quickly as possible so I could get back to her.

As I started my car, I felt a tingling on the back of my neck, almost as if someone were watching me. I glanced around but didn't see anyone lurking nearby. I spotted a figure sitting in a blue compact, but they had their head down and a phone to their ear. They were probably just finishing a conversation before going inside.

I'd been driving for almost ten minutes when my phone rang, and I answered it by pressing a button on my steering wheel.

"Where are you?" Deacon demanded.

"On my way," I reassured him. "I won't be late. Are you seriously calling to check on me, or has there been a development?"

"I think you need to turn around and return to Phoebe's place. We finally got a hit on the person stalking your woman. The reconstructed prints brought up some local junkies that had been arrested, so we looked into each of them and found a woman recently discharged from the same rehab facility as Phoebe's brother. Stephanie Dalton. We don't have a location for her yet, but she drives a blue compact." He rattled off the license plate number, and I cursed as I yanked my wheel to the left and made a quick U-turn. Thankfully the road was empty.

"I saw her car in front of Phoebe's apartment when I left."

"Fucking hell. I'll call the police and smooth things over with the brass here."

He hung up, and I raced back to the parking lot, my tires screeching as I turned in and stopped the SUV in front of the building. Not caring about anything but getting up to Phoebe, I threw the vehicle into park and leaned over to get my gun out of the glove compartment. I assembled it in seconds and shoved in a full clip before hopping out of the car, not bothering to shut my door as I ran toward Phoebe's apartment.

I grabbed the knob and twisted as I pushed, bursting inside and causing the door to slam against the wall. For a moment, the world stopped spinning, and fear like I'd never known engulfed me.

Phoebe was backed up against the wall, holding her robe tight around her as she tried to shrink herself as much as possible. A woman stood in front of her yelling and waving a big knife around. Startled by the loud crash of the door, she whipped around, nearly slicing Phoebe's arm.

The fear instantly morphed into utter rage, but my training kicked in, and I remained calm.

"Put down the knife and step away from her," I ordered. The girl blinked a few times, her bloodshot eyes glazed over. Son of a bitch. She was clearly high, which meant that what little common sense she might have possessed had probably gone out the window already.

"Who are you?" she squawked, her hands gesturing wildly.

I kept my eyes on the sharp blade as I took a slow step forward, keeping the hand holding my gun hidden behind me. "I'm Silas," I told her.

"Stay back! You're the boyfriend, aren't you?" she asked as her eyes narrowed. "She doesn't deserve you! Why should she be happy when she ruined my life?"

I didn't know exactly what story the girl had convinced herself was true, but from her comment and knowing she had been in rehab with Paul, I felt like I had a pretty clear picture of what was going on.

"Maybe you're right," I said with a sympathetic smile. "But killing her won't solve the problem. You can't be with Paul if you're in jail."

The girl laughed hysterically, and her eyes bounced around as if she couldn't keep her focus on any one thing. "When she's gone, Paul and I will run away together. He won't let anything happen to me."

The girl spun around and screamed, "She has to die!"

Before she could raise the knife, I aimed my gun and put a bullet in her shoulder.

She screamed like a banshee, and her hand flexed, dropping the knife to the ground. Phoebe scrambled to pick it up, then made a mad dash over to me. I shoved her behind my back and trained my gun on the girl's head.

"The police are on their way. Stay right there

until they get here, or you'll be going out of here in a body bag instead of a stretcher."

Phoebe clung to my back, but I couldn't focus on her until the threat was eliminated.

I sent up a silent thank you to Deacon because I heard sirens rapidly approaching. Only a minute or two later, two policemen rushed through the door. They immediately restrained Stephanie, and I allowed myself to switch my attention to my girl. I twisted around and wrapped her up in a tight embrace.

"Are you okay?" I grunted.

"Yes," she answered, her voice muffled because she'd face-planted into my shirt. "Thanks to you."

I loosened my hold on her and grasped her chin, raising her face. "Don't thank me for doing my job, baby. You're mine, and I protect what's mine."

Over the next thirty minutes, there was a flurry of chaos.

The EMTs arrived and restrained Stephanie on a stretcher. She was still screaming threats and obscenities as they carried her out the door.

The police took our statements, and between our recap of the events and the ranting of the psychotic woman, they quickly determined I'd shot her in self-defense.

We were engulfed in silence when they finally left and the door shut behind them. Phoebe burst into tears, and I scooped her up, carrying her to the couch so I could hold my girl while she cried. Eventually, her sobs subsided, and she looked up at me. "I don't want to stay here," she whispered.

"Then we won't."

Phoebe was reluctant to part from me, so I kept my arm around her as we went to her bedroom. She let go of me long enough to change into a T-shirt and shorts, then helped me pack her bags. I planned to have a few of the guys come and help me pack up her place next week and move her in with me. That way, she wouldn't ever need to step foot in this apartment again.

We headed out to my SUV, which was still idling in the middle of the parking lot, but someone had at least shut the door. I helped her inside and hurried around to climb in, then held her hand tightly in mine as I drove to my condo.

At my place, I took her hand as we walked back to the bedroom where I tossed her bags into a corner. Then I drew her close to me and dropped my head to place a lingering kiss on her lips. The adrenaline was fading, and with it, the rage and fear, leaving an overwhelming need.

She smiled softly when I released her lips and whispered, "I know you said not to thank you, but I can't help it. You saved me."

"I will always protect you, baby. I would never let anything happen to the woman I love. I can't live without you."

Phoebe's pretty eyes grew wide and round, and her jaw dropped slightly. After a beat, she sucked in a breath, then expelled it slowly. "You love me?"

I raised an eyebrow as the corners of my mouth curled down into a frown over her shock. "Of course, I love you."

Phoebe shook her head and sighed with exasperation. "How was I supposed to know that when you've never told me?"

It hit me that she was right. I'd never said the words out loud even though I'd thought them so many times. I cradled her face in my hands and stared into her eyes. "I love you."

I brushed my thumbs over the freckles on the apples of her cheeks and softly kissed her lips once more. Then I narrowed my eyes on her. "And you love me, too."

Phoebe's face lit up, and she beamed at me with a giant smile. "Of course, I love you," she said, repeating my earlier phrase.

Hearing the words from her mouth broke the last of my control. I grabbed the hem of her shirt and ripped it over her head before my mouth crashed down onto hers.

All the adrenaline and emotions bombarding us made our movements frantic and hungry. We moved toward the bed, only breaking our kisses to remove the rest of our clothing. When we stumbled against it, I swept her up with an arm under her knees and tossed her onto the mattress. I immediately climbed on and moved over her until our bodies pressed together. The feel of her silky skin sent streaks of electricity over my nerves that went straight to my dick.

She clung to me as I dropped my head to trail kisses down her neck to the tips of her breasts. I loved the sound of her sweet gasp as I wrapped my lips around one peak and tugged on it with my teeth. Her arms tightened around me, and her legs came up to circle my waist.

My cock was cradled in the apex of her thighs, and with each movement, her juices coated the shaft so I slid easily between her folds.

I switched to the other breast, and Phoebe arched her back. "Silas," she moaned.

Releasing the bud with a pop, I groaned, "I love the way you say my name."

"And I love the way you worship my body," she sighed. "But right now, I need you inside me."

She wouldn't get any argument from me. I adjusted my position, notching the tip of my cock at her opening, then I took her lips in a ravenous kiss as I thrust inside, bottoming out completely. Phoebe cried out, and her legs gripped my hips like a vise as her fingernails dug into the flesh of my shoulders.

"Fuck, yes," I hissed. "So damn tight."

I began to move and set a steady pace, fucking her fast and hard. I couldn't seem to get close enough, deep enough. I wanted to be so connected that it wasn't possible to tell where she ended and I began.

I slipped my hands under her knees and unlocked her legs from around me. Then I pushed them up toward her chest and opened them wide. The new angle allowed me to slide in so far that I bumped her cervix.

"Oh fuck, yes," I rasped. "That's it, baby. Tilt that tight little pussy and let me all the way in. Fuck, yes! Fuck!"

"Silas!" Phoebe called out as her inner muscles contracted around me. "I-I...need..."

"I know what you need, baby," I growled. "And you're gonna get it. For the rest of your life."

There was no control left. I slammed in and out of her channel like a man possessed. When she began to tremble, and I felt a telltale tingling at the base of my spine, I knew I would last much longer. "Come, baby," I demanded. "Come with me. I want to feel your pussy squeezing the fuck out of my dick, milking my cock as I fill you with my come."

Phoebe slammed her head back against the mattress and screamed as violent shudders wracked her body. The spasms massaged my shaft as I exploded inside her, sucking out what I thought was every drop. But as we both spiraled down, I realized I was still hard as a fucking baseball bat. I captured Phoebe's wrists and secured them in one of my hands above her head. Then I used the other to feed myself her tits as I picked up my pace again and pounded into my woman, knocking the headboard into the wall.

"I can't," Phoebe gasped. "Silas! Don't stop! Oh yes! Yes!"

It didn't take long to drive her back up, and I slipped a hand between us to rub her bundle of nerves. "Give me another one, Phoebe," I ordered. "Let me see you fall apart in my arms, baby."

I pinched her clit, and she shattered, screaming my name as I followed her over the edge.

"Oh fuck, Phoebe! Fuck!" I bellowed as I spurted endless amounts of hot seed into her womb.

It could have been an hour—or maybe even days—but eventually, our breathing evened out as our rapidly beating hearts slowed to a steady rhythm. All I really knew was that I was fucking exhausted, and I'd be content to lay there with Phoebe in my arms forever.

I held her against me as I rolled onto my back. She ended up sprawled across my body, and I was still buried inside her while our mixed arousal leaked from her pussy.

"Fuck," I groaned. "I didn't use a condom."

Phoebe raised her head and rolled her eyes at me. "When have you ever?"

She had a point. We'd been so caught up in each other that I'd forgotten to use protection all weekend. Not that I'd really made an effort to remember...

"Whatever happens, I'll take care of you. I love you more than anything, and I would be over the moon to start a family with you."

Phoebe's face flushed red, but she was practically glowing as she aimed a giant smile my way. "I'd like that, too."

"Great," I replied matter-of-factly. "If I haven't already knocked you up, I'll get to work on that as soon as I find the energy."

Phoebe snickered and wiggled her hips. "Feels like you're already up to the task," she sassed.

I grinned and hugged her tight to my body. "Fuck, I love you."

"Love you too, sailor."

EPILOGUE

PHOEBE

"Wow," I breathed as Silas ushered me through the front doors of the boutique hotel where we would spend the weekend. Just the two of us, for the first time since we'd had Samuel thirteen months ago.

"Good job, baby." He slid his hand from my lower back to my hip as he moved to stand next to me. "This place is fucking incredible."

A night at this hotel normally ran upward of six hundred dollars for a regular room, but our stay was being comped. The owners were new clients of my employer, and my boss had assigned me to their marketing team.

Getting pregnant so soon after starting my job had worried me, but my boss had been so understanding. She even threw me a baby shower in the office, where my coworkers all gave me a paid day off from their bank in lieu of gifts. I had been so touched that I'd bawled my eyes out, thanks to all the pregnancy hormones.

When I returned from my three months of maternity leave, she told me to expect a promotion within the next year and happily handed over several clients for me to work with on my own. I advanced to my new position last week, and along with the raise came additional clients. Luckily, it had been just in time to land this hotel since the perks were unbeatable...and I wanted to fully enjoy them while I could.

When we approached the registration desk, the man at the computer looked up and flashed us a smile. Unfortunately, his gaze then locked on my chest—and the boobs that had never returned to their original size after I gave birth to our son. Leveling a glare at the guy, Silas wrapped his fingers around my wrist and tugged me to his side. I thought he was just going to give the employee heck for daring to ogle me, but after he growled, "Keep your eyes to yourself," he led me over to the woman working at the far end of the counter.

"So sorry about that," she whispered.

"It's okay," I assured her as my husband continued to glare at her coworker.

When I gave her my name for the reservation and she pulled it up on her computer, she beamed a huge smile at me. "Oh boy, will he regret that faux pas since you work directly with the owner."

"Yup, he sure is," I confirmed with a nod. Although employee performance was outside of my purview, word of mouth was everything in marketing. It could easily be said that how their front desk staff treated customers had an impact on how effective my campaigns would be.

My grin was as big as hers when she informed me that we'd been booked into a suite with an ocean-front view. There was an added spring in my step as we made our way to the elevator.

I was excited to have my gorgeous husband all to myself for the next two days, especially somewhere we could order in room service. But this was the first time we'd left Samuel overnight, and when the doors slid shut in front of us, I started to get nervous.

As I bit my bottom lip and rapidly blinked a few times, Silas proved how well he knew me. "Will you feel better if we call your mom as soon as we get to the room?"

"Yes." I beamed a relieved smile at him. "I know

we only left him with her twenty minutes ago, and she's babysat for us plenty of times before, but this feels different."

He brushed a kiss against my temple. "You're such a good mom."

"And you're an awesome dad."

The elevator dinged, and then the doors slid open again. Silas guided me down the hallway to our suite, which was even more gorgeous than I had imagined. But I didn't take the time to appreciate my surroundings. Instead, I yanked my phone from my purse and called our boy.

My mom picked up on the first ring. "How did I know you wouldn't even last the first full hour before calling?"

"Because you're a mom, too," I quipped.

"True," she conceded, switching to video mode so I could see Samuel's chubby face as he munched on an animal cracker. "As you can see, my grandson is doing just fine. Now go enjoy your time with your husband. I'll send you lots of updates with pictures for when you're not busy."

Silas and I blew kisses at Samuel before we hung up. Then he took my phone and purse and set them on the small table in the sitting area. After yanking open the curtains so we could stare out at the ocean, he moved behind me and wrapped his arms around my front to pull me against his chest. "Two whole days with you all to myself, whatever will we do?"

His hot breath against my ear sent a shiver down my spine that only strengthened when he ground his hard-on against my butt. Turning in his arms, I fully intended to make a filthy suggestion that wouldn't surprise him at all. Instead, I blurted, "I'm pregnant."

"Pregnant?" Silas echoed, his eyes widening as his gaze dropped to my still-flat stomach.

"Uh-huh." I nodded. "I didn't notice until this morning that my period is a week late, and I still had a test in the bathroom cabinet from when we found out about Samuel. So I took it while you were getting him ready. And it was positive."

"Fuck yeah!" He picked me up and twirled me around in a circle, a huge grin on his face. "It's a good thing we have so much privacy now that we have something to celebrate."

EPILOGUE

SILAS

Quietly, I opened the door to my wife's home office. I didn't want to disturb her if she was on a call, but lucky for me, she was just powering down her computer. Stepping fully inside, I shut and locked the door behind me.

Phoebe spun around in her chair, and when she saw me, a giant smile lit up her face. "You're home!" She jumped out of the chair and threw herself into my arms.

"Fuck, I missed you," I grunted before taking her lips in a passionate kiss. I'd been gone for two weeks and had arrived home this afternoon, just in time to pick up Samuel from preschool and Carly from her playdate.

As I devoured Phoebe's mouth, I walked her backward and spun us around so I could sit in her chair. Then I yanked her down into my lap and settled her with her legs hanging on either side of mine.

Phoebe tore her lips away and glanced at the door, panting, "Where are the kids?"

"Paul and Emily took them to dinner and a movie."

Two years after Paul finished rehab, he met the love of his life. Emily was amazing and had her shit together, so she told his ass straight out that if he wanted her, he'd have to walk the straight and narrow. He'd agreed, and a year later, they were married.

They were expecting their own little bundle of joy in three months, and they loved to "practice" by taking our kids off our hands.

Which worked out perfectly since I was on a mission to knock up my wife again.

Thirty minutes later, I shoved Phoebe's ripped panties into my pocket and helped her back into her shorts. When I tucked myself back in and zipped up my jeans, I didn't bother to button them or put my shirt back on.

"Are you finished for the day?" I asked as I

curled my arm around her and hauled her up against my body.

"Finished working or finished coming?" she sassed.

"Baby, I know you're not finished coming," I growled playfully as I grabbed her ass and boosted her up so she put her legs around my waist.

I carried her to our bedroom, where I ate her pussy before filling it full of my seed again.

Much later, I rolled over and flopped back onto the mattress beside her, breathing hard. "If that didn't do it, then I'll probably die before I manage to knock you up again."

"I think you may have killed me this time," Phoebe giggled. "I can't move a muscle. Good thing I'm already pregnant."

A burst of energy shot through my body, and I jackknifed up in bed. "You're pregnant?" I shouted.

Phoebe nodded and laughed. "You can't be surprised by this...you filled me with so much come the week before you left that it was still dripping out of me days later."

"Nah," I muttered with an arrogant grin. "Not surprised, baby. Proud. My boys worked fucking fast."

My wife rolled her eyes, but she was smiling

happily. "If your head gets any bigger, you won't be able to walk through doorways anymore."

"Samuel's been asking for a baby brother since we brought Carly home from the hospital," I chuckled.

"Hopefully, he won't throw too big of a tantrum if it's a girl."

"You know," I drawled. "I've heard that you're more likely to get a boy if—"

"Mommy! Daddy! We're home!" our little boy shouted.

"Hold that thought," I quipped. "We'll try out those techniques later."

Phoebe raised an eyebrow. "And if I want another girl?"

I grinned and leaned down to give her a quick, hard kiss. "We'll try all those, too. Whatever it takes, baby."

She laughed as we both climbed out of bed to dress and go greet our little ones.

As we walked out of the bedroom door, I smacked my wife's perfect ass. "Love you more every damn day, baby."

Phoebe stopped and looked back at me over her shoulder, her eyes swimming with tears as she sniffled, "Don't say stuff like that to me right now."

I couldn't help laughing because I remembered how emotional she'd been during the last two pregnancies. She glared at me for a moment, then laughed along with me.

"Seriously, what is with these hormones?" she muttered as she continued down the hall.

I reached out and grabbed her arm, swinging her around and plastering her body up against mine. "I think you meant to say. 'I love you, too, Silas.'"

Phoebe went up on her tiptoes and kissed me before whispering, "I love you more than anything, husband."

I grinned. "That's even better."

When we met our babies in the foyer, I watched my family talk and smile, basking in the love filling our home.

Phoebe liked to joke that she'd been claimed by the sailor. But the truth was, I'd been hers from the first second our eyes met. And we'd belong to each other forever.

Just in case you missed it, Kade got his happily ever after in Owned by the Officer, and Huntley, Merrick, and Deacon's stories are all available in Black Ops: Volume 1!

If you sign up for our newsletter, we'll send you a FREE ebook copy of The Virgin's Guardian, which you can't get anywhere else!

ABOUT THE AUTHOR

The writing duo of Elle Christensen and Rochelle Paige team up under the Fiona Davenport pen name to bring you sexy, insta-love stories filled with alpha males. If you want a quick & dirty read with a guaranteed happily ever after, then give Fiona Davenport a try!

For all the STEAMY news about Fiona's upcoming releases... sign up for our newsletter!

Printed in Great Britain
by Amazon

21716158R00081